SKIN DEEP

SKIN DEEP

GUY GARCIA

UNIVERSITY OF CALIFORNIA PRESS
Berkeley · Los Angeles · London

For my parents,
for their parents,
and for Cathleen

University of California Press
Berkeley and Los Angeles, California

University of California Press, Ltd.
London, England

First Paperback Printing 1997

Library of Congress Cataloging-in-Publication Data
Garcia, Guy, 1955–
    Skin deep / Guy Garcia.
        p.   cm. — (California fiction)
    ISBN 0-520-20836-6
    1. Detective and mystery stories. gsafd.   I. Title.   II. Series.
PS3557.A67S55 1997
813'.54—DC20   96-34570
                                                          CIP

Printed in the United States of America
Designed by Jack Harrison

1   2   3   4   5   6   7   8   9

The paper used in this publication meets the minimum requirements of
American National Standard for Information Sciences—Permanence
of Paper for Printed Library Materials, ANSI Z39.48-1984. ∞

SKIN DEEP

Josefina Juárez is praying as the Number 19 bus lurches to a stop at the corner of Whittier and Atlantic, deep in the East Los Angeles barrio. She clutches a string of small black beads, letting them slip through her fingers one at a time.

O Santísima Señora, reina del cielo y de la tierra. Madre de Dios, óyeme . . .

For the third time since boarding the connecting bus on Santa Monica Boulevard she pulls her white knitted shawl tighter around her slim shoulders. Across the graffiti-marked seats, cryptogrammic letters declare that LUDE LADY LOVES ELECTRIC VATO.

. . . Madre buenísima, oye mis pecados, no me dejes sola en esta hora de mi esperanza . . .

"You don't think you can hog it all to yourself now, do you?" A bovine woman points to the empty seat next to Josefina. "Comprende, miss?"

The darkening of Josefina's face shows that she understands. But instead of moving over, she grabs her shopping bag and hurries to the exit. It isn't until she is out on the street, a cloud of exhaust stinging her nostrils, that she dares to lift her head. Our Lady of Guadalupe is three blocks away. She can see it, next to the Friendship Motors car dealership. Behind that is the church parking lot where the Sisters hold their Easter bazaar every spring. Josefina squeezes her rosary

3

and remembers the first time she ever saw the arched windows and pseudo-Colonial bell tower. The gaudy air of confusion, the squeals of laughing children, the strolling dark-haired men in their starched white shirts, the earthy aromas of pozole, menudo, frijoles, and fresh tortillas had drawn her there, like a fly to manteca. The scene was a mirage to her, at once familiar and terribly removed from the pockmarked streets of her tiny village near Zihuatánejo, Mexico.

She found herself that day in front of a booth displaying crucifixes on braided silver chains, St. Christopher medals, and gleaming black rosaries. The Sister inside the booth asked if she would like to take a closer look at something. Josefina shook her head and smiled. The fifty dollars crumpled in her purse would have to last until she found a job and a place to live. "It's a sin for a pretty girl like you to look so sad," the Sister said gently. She was about Josefina's age, and there was something playful in her smile. Before she knew it, Josefina was recounting the tale of her trek north, including the death of her mother, her unhappy stay with relatives in the desolate outskirts of Mexico City, her decision to cross the border and start a new life in the United States. Then came the clandestine arrangements, the hasty goodbyes, and the crowded ride in the back of a truck carrying construction supplies. Josefina had heard the horror stories of robbery and murder, of entire families left in the middle of nowhere to die or be found by the border police, but Josefina had made up her mind. If I stay here I'm already dead, she told herself, and so she had showed up at the appointed place and time and paid three hundred American dollars to be shoved into the back of a truck with a young couple from Sinaloa named Julio and Rosa and half a dozen other nervous strangers. It was almost dawn when the coyote had halted at a Greyhound bus station somewhere outside Bakersfield and ordered everyone out. Josefina joined the others as they huddled against the building, momentarily blinded by the glare of the truck's headlights. Then the coyote was gone and the immigrants were left alone to peer at the black horizon while a bloodshot sun ignited the desert.

When the bus left them off in L.A., Julio and Rosa asked Josefina to come with them to their uncle's strawberry farm in the Sacramento Valley. Looking around at the lounging derelicts and rows of grimy plastic chairs, Josefina was tempted to accept. But then she remembered the way Julio had pressed his leg against hers in the noisy blackness of the truck and decided to take her chances alone. Besides, she was planning to stay with the cousin of a friend of her aunt's. The cousin worked as a dressmaker in the downtown textile district and could help her find a job. Josefina had barely taken twenty steps when a squat woman in nice clothes approached her. She handed Josefina a card with a telephone number on it and told her in Spanish to call her when she was ready to make money. Then she offered to help Josefina find the right bus connection and squeezed her hand with a businesslike firmness before walking away.

During the ride out to East L.A., Josefina had been struck by the indiscriminate affluence of her new surroundings. She had never seen so many cars outside of Mexico City. But she did not know how to drive and thanked God for the buses, which reminded her of home. Once in the barrio, Josefina needed another forty-five minutes to find the right address, only to learn that the cousin had moved away. The girl had apparently run off with her boyfriend. Josefina walked the streets in a daze, letting her feet find their own direction. She wandered past taco stands and furniture stores, past Garfield High and Millie's Bar, ignoring the whistles of men drinking beer on the corner, blind and deaf to everything except the desperate sound of her own prayers. That was when she had stumbled on the bazaar.

When Josefina finished her story, the nun took her by the hand and led her to another booth, where a fat lady in a flowered dress was selling raffle tickets for a Whirlpool washer and dryer. The woman introduced herself as Doña Sánchez and told Josefina she could stay at her house until she found a job or a husband.

"Whichever comes first," she added with a snort. The next day Josefina called the number that the woman at the bus terminal had given her. A man answered and, after a long wait, gave Josefina a second phone number. This time a girl with a Spanish accent answered in English and then switched to Spanish when Josefina identified herself. The girl's name was Marta and she said she worked at a house where they needed temporary help right away. She asked Josefina a few questions about housekeeping and gave her an address where she was expected the following morning.

The next day, when she got off the bus in Beverly Hills, Josefina finally understood that the rumors about America's unthinkable wealth were true. At first she was so intimidated by the size of the house that she could barely ring the bell, but Marta took pains to put her at ease, explaining that Josefina would be doing some of the cleaning while the more experienced maids helped with a party. Josefina did exactly as instructed, buffing the bathroom faucets until they shone like mirrors. Obviously pleased, Marta told her to come back the next day, and before long Josefina was in charge of the whole upstairs of the house. The job paid eighty dollars a week, a fantastic sum in Mexico but here just enough to buy food and clothes, repay Doña Sánchez, and rent the small room over her garage on Hubbard Street.

Josefina was happy, or at least she was no longer unhappy. In the daytime she toiled in a dreamland of luxury; at night she escaped into the make-believe reality of the novellas she bought every week from the crippled man who ran the bookstore next to the Mexican bakery. Josefina would spend hours poring over the picture-filled pages, losing herself in the heartbreaking romances of attractive strangers. She went on that way for months, suspended between the two worlds, living a furtive, solitary existence, until her life changed again.

Josefina is directly opposite the church now. As she draws nearer, her heartbeat quickens. Our Lady of Guadalupe does not look the same as it did on that bright morning almost a year ago. Trash is scattered on the cement steps and someone has ripped a gaping hole in the chain-link fence. She crosses the street like a supplicant, nearly oblivious to the screech of braking tires. "Fucking wetback," the driver shouts. "Go get run over in your own country!" In her haste to enter the building, she doesn't notice a second car pass slowly and slide into a parking space a few hundred feet up the block.

With a sigh of relief, Josefina enters the cool dark vestibule. Lifting the shawl over her hair, she kneels and crosses herself before the altar, then moves to a small table with votive candles and long wooden matches. Josefina takes a candle and a match, making sure to leave a quarter in the tarnished metal collection box. The statue of the Virgin stands enclosed in its own shrine in a darkened corner, illuminated by a battery of glowing tributes. Each wavering flame represents a burning desire, an unfulfilled wish, an act of hope against despair. As a hundred shadows dance on the wall behind her, Josefina carefully places the candle in a red glass cup and lights it. Then she kneels at the padded railing and holds the rosary against her lips.

. . . *Santa María, Madre de Dios, ruega por nosotros pecadores, ahora y en la hora de nuestra muerte* . . .

As the two men block the light from the street behind her, Josefina prays for her dead parents and her unborn brothers and sisters. She prays for her friends and for her enemies. She prays for her soul and for the souls of all others. She prays for her life.

1

The sermon on the steps of St. Patrick's Cathedral was just beginning as David Loya turned east on Fiftieth Street and continued to walk briskly through midtown New York City. Holding the battered Bible to his chest, the sidewalk preacher tugged at his scum-stained collar and cleared his throat.

"The fat rats of the city shall inherit what's left of the earth," he bellowed, raising his tattered sleeves in an asymmetrical cross. ". . . Behold the vermin of Bloomingdale's, the sybarites of Saks . . ."

David had heard this speech a dozen times before, uttered through a pious froth of spittle and alcohol-induced dementia. The reactions of passersby, he had noticed, usually fell into two distinct categories: that of the hardened New Yorkers, who never even acknowledged the existence of their wrathful accuser, and that of the tourists, who either cowered along the opposite edge of the sidewalk or gathered around like patrons at an amusement arcade sideshow. The crowds seemed to grow and shrink in direct proportion to the evangelist's condemnatory zeal, which usually peaked during the Christmas rush. But it was early September now, and David was late for work.

". . . Yea, they who walk in the shadow of unlimited credit shall be cast down, down to the fires that rage beneath Macy's bargain basement . . ."

David's mind was still fuzzy from too much drink and not enough sleep. Scenes from the night before came back to him sharply etched. Was it last night or the week before? It didn't much matter. Only the names and details varied in what had become a depressingly familiar scenario. There was usually some art opening for one of Andrea's star painters, then dinner at a restaurant where the patrons are outnumbered by oversized cacti or mirrors or crumbling Corinthian columns. As they eat, several people approach the table and snap their picture without bothering to ask for permission. David notices that the artist, no matter how insouciant, never fails to stop mid-bite or mid-sentence and pose for the camera. After the obligatory tour of East Village nightclubs, they all end up at the artist's SoHo loft, where David's attention is drawn to a large—or perhaps an extremely small—work-in-progress. The center of the canvas is taken up by a black hole or a marble pillar on fire or a cartoonish drawing of Mickey Mouse masturbating. As David stands there, drinking, staring, wondering when they can go home, he hears footsteps behind him. "What do you think?" the artist asks as he places his hand on the back of David's neck or his arm or the small of his back. "It's a perfect marriage of form and content," David answers, annoyed by the slur in his speech and the gentle pressure of the man's fingers. "And I'd appreciate it if you kept your slimy paw off me." The artist laughs and glances toward the living room. "Andrea is included, of course," he explains, as if this somehow makes it all right. Later, in the cab, Andrea accuses David of being "typically rude." David replies she should be thankful he didn't punch the guy out.

Her mouth is hard as she speaks to the window. "That would be just like you," she says.

"That would be just like me," he repeats.

*　　*　　*

9

A panel of refracted sunlight caught David in the eyes and made him blink. He looked at his watch: 9:30. His colleagues would already be at their desks, sorting documents for the court date that afternoon. The firm they were defending, an imperious conglomerate called Dynagroup, had been accused of interfering with the satellite transmissions of a rival company. Two weeks ago, the plaintiff had dumped three thousand pages of discovery on David's team and he had since spent so many hours reading about modems and microbits and errant wavelengths that he was sure he was about to blow a fuse himself. Worst of all, the case could conceivably drag on for years, certainly long enough to render the technology at stake obsolete. The irony of the situation was almost more than David could bear. His single attempt to share this subversive insight with his colleagues had been cut short by uncomprehending stares.

"You're a lawyer," someone had pointedly reminded him. "Not a judge."

David's building slanted overhead at an impossible angle, slicing the sky into geometric patterns. At least it's Friday, he told himself. By noon, after a briefing from his secretary and a couple of cups of coffee, he would be ready to deal with the rest of the day. Not that his presence made any difference; the briefs and meetings and citations seemed to have a will of their own. The wheels of justice would continue to turn with or without him. All he had to do was join their inexorable motion for a few hours. With luck, it would keep him too busy to think about the implications of what he was, or wasn't, doing. It had gotten to the point lately where even his biweekly paycheck couldn't cheer him up.

Passing through the Italian pink-marble lobby, David stepped into the elevator and, as the doors clamped shut, remembered a dream from the night before:

He is standing in the same elevator, avoiding, as always, the eyes of his fellow passengers, who are reflected as blurry phantoms on its stainless-steel walls. Somewhere between ground level and the first express stop on the twenty-fifth floor the elevator lurches to a halt. After a moment of consternation, David and seven strangers are suddenly forced to acknowledge one another in suffocating intimacy. Surprise gives way to annoyance and anger; then, as the minutes tick by, fear and panic. Across the elevator car David notices a girl with long black hair watching him. She presses up against him; they have made a silent pact to help each other escape. Her lips are inches from his ear as she whispers a plan. People are beginning to scream and push. An old woman's cheek is bleeding. Amid the confusion, David and the girl somehow manage to climb out through the trapdoor in the ceiling. As they scale the ladder in the elevator shaft, David smells salt air and hears seagulls crying. He reaches the door to the roof, but it won't budge. The girl joins him and they heave together. The door bursts open.

"Getting out, please."

David returned to reality just in time to avoid missing his floor. Moments later his secretary, Sarah, filled him in on the morning's events, ticking off his schedule in her efficient Boston twang.

"You have four client calls," she briskly informed him. "The Dynagroup hearing is this afternoon at 3:30. You've got a group conference at 2:00, and I hope whatever you did last night was worth it. I told everyone you had a dentist appointment." He willed himself to look amused. "Oh, and the old man wants to see you in his office pronto."

The last bit of news made him uneasy. There had been a recent slew of firings, each of which had been preceded by a visit to Mr. Metcalf's office. He had been summoned by his boss only twice since starting with the firm two years ago. The first time was to be told he had been hired. The second was for a raise. He didn't think he was due for another one.

David looked at his secretary and said, "You're an angel."

"In what sense?" she asked.

David knocked on the heavy door. He could still see the look on his mother's face the day he became one of the few East Los Angeles Chicanos ever to graduate from Harvard Law School. "My hijo the lawyer," she had said in an awe-struck whisper, her eyes brimming with tears.

David heard a murmur of admittance from behind the inch and a half of polished mahogany.

"You asked to see me, sir?"

Even the most trivial act of deference made David feel slightly diminished. Despite Harvard Law, despite his in-come and position, his sensitivity to any kind of implied subservience was never far from the surface. However, he quickly learned not to take such minor humiliations per-sonally. Paying lip service to superiors was as intrinsic to the corporate culture as expense accounts and two-hour lunches. It was all part of the formula necessary to break out of the pack, to climb another rung of the organizational ladder. If David had ever been a victim of discrimination, he had not been aware of it. Of course, the combination of a Spanish surname and impeccable academic credentials hadn't hurt, but he found the idea of making allowances for some-one because of their name or the shade of their skin totally abhorrent. David steadfastly believed his rapid advance into the upper echelons of his profession had much more to do with the fact that his talents were equal to or better than his colleagues at the firm. If he had any expectations, it was only to be treated exactly the same as everyone else. Armed with innate intelligence and the ambition drilled into him by his parents, David had come very far indeed, and it seemed that there was no limit to how much further he could go. In fact, if he played his cards right, he figured he had a decent shot at a partnership within the next couple of years. It was only a matter of diligence and hard work. Any guilt he might have once felt about "selling out" for a big-bucks job had long ago been replaced by the conviction that the most useful thing he could do for his people was to fulfill the promise of his own success and thereby set an example for others to follow. Once, at the end of a particularly grueling all-nighter, David had looked out of his office window to see a single balloon riding the draft between two skyscrapers. As the balloon floated in the limpid dawn, David had identified with its upward trajectory, powered by natural forces in a solitary, self-contained ascent.

Metcalf wordlessly motioned for David to take a seat. "Mr. Loya, you are a bright young attorney," he began, and then stopped, as if letting the obvious sink in for a moment. "I've seen a lot of bright young attorneys come through that door. Sharp. Ambitious. Like you. Most of them didn't have a future here."

A part of David's mind returns to the dream. The door in the elevator shaft opens to reveal a long white beach. The jungle behind it is the color of wet jade. Off in the distance, huts of dried leaves dot the sand.

"Do you know why, Mr. Loya?" Metcalf was asking.

"No, sir."

"Because they were too sharp, too bright. Tripped on their own tails, as it were."

Metcalf had the self-satisfied air of someone who had neatly solved a difficult puzzle. He picked a piece of lint off his charcoal suit, and as he spoke again, David had the disconcerting conviction that, to Metcalf, his attentive employee and the speck of dust between his fingers had become indistinguishable. Metcalf shifted his weight and stretched his neck out to scrutinize a single sheet of paper on his desk.

"I see that you were scheduled for two weeks' vacation beginning next week."

"That's correct, sir."

"Which you have canceled." Metcalf focused his eyes sharply. "Why, Mr. Loya?"

The question caught David totally by surprise. "Well, sir, I . . . We're very much still in the heat of litigation. It seemed irresponsible for me . . ."

13

"That's a lot of crap, Mr. Loya, and we both know it."

David tried to form words with his lips, but no sound emerged.

"You know as well as I do that this case could drag on for years." There was something akin to mockery in the old man's expression. "I think the firm will survive until you get back from . . . wherever. You've been on the Dynagroup case nearly, let's see, six months. I think it's time you let someone else bear the brunt for a while."

David can feel the hot sun on his skin, hear the crashing waves.

"I'm not sure that I follow, sir."

"Then I'll make it perfectly plain for you. I'm suggesting, no, I'm *telling* you to take this vacation. Your mind hasn't been on your work lately. It's perfectly natural for the brain to become addled by a case of this, ah, complexity. Think of it as a mandatory leave of absence—with pay, of course."

David can taste the ocean salt on his lips.

"May I make a suggestion, Mr. Loya?"

"Of course, sir."

"Find a place with no telephones. There are tons of them in the back pages of *The New Yorker*. Or, better yet, my secretary can suggest something. I hear Bora Bora is 'in' this year. When you return you will be refreshed and ready to reapply yourself wholeheartedly to your work. Do we understand each other, Mr. Loya?"

"Absolutely. Thank you, sir."

"You're welcome, Mr. Loya."

David's expression remained neutral as he rose and retraced his steps to the door. It was only when he was safely back in the corridor that he allowed himself to exhale.

Like a vulture smelling blood in the air, Bragin was hovering over David's desk. "Don't tell me they've made you partner," he said casually.

"Not unless we're opening an office in Antigua."

Bragin's features narrowed with interest. "What's that supposed to mean?"

"That means mind your own business."

"Sorry I bothered to ask. I'll see you at the meeting."

"Right."

David settled into his chair, already regretting his outburst; it would only give Bragin more grist for the gossip mill. David picked up the phone. Andrea answered on the third ring.

"Is there some particular reason you always wait until the third ring?" he said without saying hello.

"Well, two is too eager, four is too late."

"I can't believe anyone notices that sort of thing."

"You did. Besides, you didn't call to discuss my phone-answering technique, did you? I've given up hoping you might have wanted to apologize for last night."

"I've got something a little more important on my mind just now."

"Hold on a sec."

He could hear her ordering her Dominican maid to do something rápidamente. Her Spanish was pretty good. Better than his, in fact.

"Look, I'm as sorry about the way the evening turned out as you—maybe more so. Let's just forget it, okay?"

"Forgotten. But that's not . . ."

There was more jabbering in the background.

"I'm sorry, sweetheart. What were you saying?" Her voice had that slightly breathless quality that either aroused or annoyed him, depending on the circumstances.

"I'm being forced to take a vacation."

"Is that bad?"

"That depends."

"On what?"

"On you."

"David, what's wrong?"

"Nothing. Nothing at all."

He could sense her impatience in the silence that followed. David decided to try a different approach.

"Maybe Metcalf is right," he said with synthetic cheer. "I

need to get out of here for a while, away from the city. I have this vision of two people running on a long white beach. The water is blue, the sun is shining, and this goddamned city is two thousand miles away. The best part about it is that the two people look just like you and me."

He could visualize her on the other end of the line: head slightly bent, blond curls cascading over delicately boned shoulders, perfect breasts tenting the gray cashmere he'd given her for her birthday. He could almost feel her long fingers wrapped around the receiver, smell her scent. But try as he might, he could not picture the expression on her face.

"Was I just hallucinating?" he said into the mouthpiece.

"Don't be absurd, David. It's just that you know I can't. The opening is two weeks away. Look, we've been through all this already. That's why you put your vacation off in the first place, remember?"

"All too well. Except that it's not the first place, it's the second place. If we postpone Antigua again, it'll be the third place."

"David, can we talk about this later?"

"Maybe your philosophy is off a notch. Maybe three rings is too late."

"What?"

"Figure it out."

"David, listen to me. I'll make it up to you, sweetheart." It was her seductive voice, the little-girl voice that always got to him. "I'd laugh if I didn't think you were actually serious."

"How serious does it have to be?" He was surprised by his own anger.

"I realize this hasn't been your day, but aren't you being a little melodramatic?"

"Everyone else in your life is melodramatic, why can't I do it for a change? Just because I don't wear black for breakfast or have spiked hair, or show up at the gallery with paint strategically splattered on my designer jeans?"

The happy figures in the postcard began to recede. He knew now that if he was going anywhere in the next few days, it would be alone.

"Maybe we both need a change of pace," she said stiffly.

Bragin, a secretary, and two of the other attorneys assigned to Dynagroup were already seated when he barged into the conference room.

"Sorry I'm late."

"Litigation is never having to say you're sorry," Bragin intoned.

Becker, a gangling, baby-faced Midwesterner who favored bow ties and Brooks Brothers suits, and Pearce, a laconic philatelist known for ruthlessness in and out of the courtroom, nodded and waited for David to take his place at the table. Despite the obvious disparity in their personalities, Pearce and Becker were particularly good at negotiating out-of-court settlements. Their assignment to the team had given David grounds to hope that common sense remained an option.

"Have you guys read my memo?"

"It's right here." Becker tapped the manila folder in front of him. "Nice work, Dave."

"So you guys agree that an out-of-court settlement is the only sane course of action."

Bragin tried his best to sound apologetic. "Ah, nobody said *that*, David."

"Then what *are* you saying?"

"Nobody has changed their mind about taking this to court," Pearce said evenly. "That has been the firm's position right from the start."

"And what's your position?"

"You've had your say, David," Pearce snapped. "We have

our marching orders. We can discuss it again when you get back."

"Get back from where?" David asked.

There was an uncomfortable silence in the room. Then something clicked in David's brain, like a transistor closing a circuit. "This was a setup, wasn't it?"

The secretary stopped taking notes and put down her pen, as if David had suddenly begun speaking gibberish.

"You guys were in cahoots with Metcalf right from the start, weren't you?" David continued with growing indignation. "And this so-called vacation means I'm getting my hands slapped for refusing to toe the party line."

"That's one way of looking at it," Pearce admitted dryly.

"Does anyone want to propose another way?" David demanded. "You sneaky, back-stabbing sons-of-bitches!"

He looked around the table for the slightest sign of moral support, but Bragin had turned to stare out the window.

Becker looked at his watch and frowned.

"David, you're a lawyer . . ." Pearce began.

"I know, I know," David said. "Not a judge."

It didn't take David long to clean off his desk, brief Bragin on his section of the case, and trade parting jabs with Sarah. A few minutes later he was downstairs in the echoing lobby. There had been a time not long before when nothing in the world looked more glamorous or important to him, when nothing mattered more than fitting in. Catching a glimpse of his reflection in the plate-glass window, David grimaced at the sight of his custom-made suit. There was a time when trying on an Armani jacket had given him an almost physical thrill. Now it seemed like just one more accessory in a wardrobe of ill-fitting conceits.

In the revolving door David noticed a colleague smiling

at him and he reflexively averted his eyes. The last thing he wanted to do right now was get trapped in a round of idle banter, inevitably ending with a clammy handshake and disingenuous promise to get together for lunch or an evening game of racquetball. "My girl," David muttered under his breath, "will call your girl."

Out on the sidewalk, David stood for a while absorbing the mindless rush of midday activity. Then he loosened his tie and began to walk. As David deftly wove his way through the phalanx of pinstriped businessmen, he wondered if he had begun to look like them under their button-down collars and button-down lives, under the smart veneer of their weekend tans and their weekend families and their weekend dreams.

He reached the Fifth Avenue corner where the prophet of profit had counted his nickels and his blessings, then turned south, past the window-shoppers and the wealthy matrons rubbing shoulders with blind beggars and ad executives, past the syringe-like spire of the Empire State Building and the commercial DMZ above Fourteenth Street, where the city leveled out toward the acid flashback of Greenwich Village and the self-conscious extremities of SoHo and TriBeCa.

A cab was blowing its horn, trapped in the middle of the intersection by a stampeding herd of pedestrians. The car nudged through the crowd, cutting off a well-dressed woman who defiantly slammed her purse down on the hood and kept walking. In an instant, the driver had jumped out of his seat, taken a few quick strides, and cuffed the woman on the head. "How dare you," she screamed in self-righteous horror. "He hit me!"

David, like everyone else, was too surprised to move.

"That's my car, you ofay bitch," the driver bellowed. "You don't mess with my car!"

As if by some secret agreement, four men with briefcases began advancing toward the driver.

"I never touched your car," the woman yelled back. "Why doesn't somebody do something!"

For an instant the cabbie seemed about to stand his ground; then, registering the sea of white faces around him, he beat a hasty retreat.

"Nobody fucks with my car," he shouted one last time, like a wounded animal. Then he drove off, leaving skid marks on the street.

By now a policeman had arrived. The woman was telling the officer how the cabbie had attacked her without provocation. She looked around and caught David's eye. "You saw it, didn't you?" she said, pointing to David.

"I didn't see anything," David said.

The lights were still on inside Andrea's gallery when he got there. Oversized canvases lay stacked against the walls. David couldn't see them clearly, but they seemed to be representations of natural calamities—tornadoes, blizzards, earthquakes.

In the blank-walled office, Tomi, Andrea's partner, was talking to a woman dressed in a man's suit. "That's totally irrelevant, darling," Tomi was saying. "Leonardo was the Pope's right arm, and he painted naked boys."

"Where's Andrea?"

"Out with a client," Tomi answered without turning around.

"Obviously. Any idea when she'll be back?"

"When will minimalism be back?"

"Does minimalism have a favorite restaurant?"

"Try Verdi's."

He found her there, sitting at a corner booth with an emaciated man whom David had seen on the cover of *Artforum*. At the center of each table was a rose trapped in a frozen beam of light. The artist had just drawn something on a napkin that made Andrea laugh. The napkin would probably end up in a museum someday. In an effort to keep things civil, David stayed at the bar, ordered a Heineken, and waited for Andrea to look up from her endive salad. After a few minutes, she spotted him and excused herself. It didn't help his mood any that she looked terrific.

"I hope you came here to apologize."

"I came here to talk."

"This is not the time or place."

"There never is a time or place anymore. That's the problem."

"Why do I always feel like I'm surrounded by land mines when I'm talking with you?"

"You're the one who steps on them."

"David, you're being a total jerk about this. I already told you, I'm not going to Antigua or anywhere else next week. You know perfectly well why, and it's very selfish of you to keep insisting. Then, instead of waiting for me at the loft, you come in here acting like a jealous boyfriend. Your timing really stinks."

"I'm sorry this conversation doesn't fit into your schedule. That's why I'm here and that's why I won't quietly go away and obediently wait at home for you like that six-hundred-dollar neutered dog of yours." The fact that he was fond of the beast only made David feel like more of a heel.

The artist was craning his head around to see what was taking Andrea so long. David shot him a homicidal look and the man's head snapped back like a rubber doll's. Under any other circumstances David would have laughed.

"What do you want from me?"

"I want more," he said.

It had happened: they were making a scene. Andrea was getting that about-to-cry look in her eyes. He wanted to give in, to apologize and take her in his arms before it was too late. But something in him wouldn't let go, wouldn't relent.

It was like pulling at a thread, only to find that something much bigger had begun to unravel.

"There is no more. Not right now, anyway. Don't push it. Please."

As she spoke, she seemed unbelievably fragile, as if any moment she might break into a hundred tiny pieces.

"Funny," David said, "you already sound a thousand miles away."

"That's because I'm not sure I know you anymore."

"Did you ever?"

His question was the last straw, the ultimate infidelity. Worse than indifference or another lover. Worse than a lie, because it was the truth.

She turned her head away.

"I can't even talk to you anymore."

He was reaching out to touch her when she got up off the stool and walked back to the table.

"I'm sorry," he said, without knowing why.

David drifted aimlessly through the streets, stopping every once in a while at a bar to dial Andrea's number and down a quick beer. He wound up on a bench in Washington Square Park. The images of the past year flickered through his mind over and over again: the first time he ever saw her, at a New Year's Eve loft party, the delicious moment of mutual discovery, their midnight kiss, staying up all night and toasting the sunrise in Central Park with a bottle of champagne, a winter weekend in Montauk when they never left the bedroom of their cabin. Then the dizzying dance of parties and dinners, the complacent months of steady dating, their increasingly frequent arguments, the mounting frustration with his job and with himself. The picture was clear enough, but the sound track was garbled. If there were subtitles, he couldn't read them.

"Hey, check it out: Crack. Speed. Weed. Hash. Mescaline and L.S.D."

He became cognizant of figures moving in the shadows under the trees. There were voices as well. Exhortations. Urgent whispers. Incantations to the chemical gods.

"Hey, mister! Check it out. Anything you want, I got."

The voice was closer, younger than the others. David turned to see a boy of about twelve perched on the bench next to him.

"I've got the best crack and speed in the whole park. Just ask for Mouse. Anytime after dark. Never rip you off. Cross my heart and hope to O.D."

David shook his head. "No thanks. Not tonight."

"Ah, man, don't look so sad. Things can't be that bad."

"What makes you so sure?"

"You don't live around here, do you?"

"No. Uptown."

"I know 'cause I never seen you before. I know everybody. Everybody knows me."

The dealer regarded him in silence for a moment. "Hold this. I'll be right back."

Before David could refuse, Mouse was gone, swallowed by the tribe of shilling specters. David resisted the temptation to open the small plastic wrapper, rejected the impulse to throw it away. The possibility that he was being framed crossed his mind.

Before he could decide what to do, the boy was back.

" 'Preciate, mister. An honest honky is hard to find."

"Tell me something," David asked. "How did you know I wouldn't steal the bag?"

"You're not here for drugs. Any fool worth his scratch could see that."

"Oh yeah? What am I here for?"

"If I knew that"—the boy flashed an iridescent smile—"I woulda already sold it to you."

It was after midnight by the time David circled back to Times Square, where Broadway and Seventh Avenue intersect in a seizure of noise and neon. Six years before he had stood in exactly the same spot during a two-day layover on his way to Harvard. It had been an awesome sight to a young scholarship student from East Los Angeles who was too naïve to know—as he did now—that the better parts of the city were elsewhere, anywhere in fact but Times Square, where human flotsam beached itself in front of discount electronics outlets and marquees that blared VIRGIN SLUTS IN 3-D. The heady mix of grime and glitz had reminded David of the seedy amusement parks that he had hung around in as a boy. But there had been something else there, too, something at once frightening and exhilarating; a vortex of light and energy that told David he was standing at the crossroads not only of the world but of his own future.

"It's high time to face the glorious light of a new day, amigo."

"You've got the wrong number, pal," David managed to slur, but he had already registered the jocular baritone, the ingratiating habit of stressing the wrong syllable in a word and yet making it sound somehow correct.

"Is that any way to talk to your old college chum?" Kurt Randall asked in phony reproach. "Don't tell me this big-shot New York lawyer has gotten too important to remember his erstwhile partner in disorganized crime and fellow high-income practitioner of the lowest common denominator."

"Randall, you fast-talking flake. Why can't you ever call at an hour fit for human consciousness?"

"That's really funny, Loya, because where I'm sitting, the nearest chronometer reads 9:30 a.m.—Pacific Standard Time."

"Shit," David said, looking at his own clock. There was no way of knowing when exactly he had dragged himself home and into bed. He was fairly certain, however, that it was long after his visit to Times Square, which had been followed by an intense debate over the Giants with the bartender of at least one joint called the Blarney Stone. Then a cold gust from New Jersey had steered him toward Sixth Avenue and into the waiting arms of an overzealous prostitute. He was half-seriously negotiating a mutually acceptable price when, out of nowhere, a lone cab had come to his rescue like a moral cavalry arriving just in the nick of time.

Randall's voice was still ringing in David's ear.

"Believe it or not, *mon frère*, there's a compelling *raison d'être* for this cross-continental wake-up call."

"Oh, really?" David asked as he tried to prop his throbbing head on a pillow. "And what might that be?"

"Well, as silly as it sounds, I need your advice on a legal matter."

David was instantly wide awake. "You're not in some kind of trouble or something?"

"No trouble, but possibly 'something.' I wanted you to recommend someone on the West Coast with reliable legal expertise. Someone I can trust to have good judgment and, most importantly, to keep their mouth shut. You wouldn't know anyone who fits that bill, would you, pal?"

"A trustworthy lawyer? No such animal."

"Ah," Kurt intoned. "That's what I figured."

"Except for me, of course."

"Of course. But you know what they say about long-distance relationships ..."

"They never work out."

"That's what she said."

"You know," David casually suggested, "you could just tell me about it over the phone." He was trying his best not to sound too interested.

"Well, not really, amigo. It's a bit complicated—and confidential. I'm sure you understand."

"Understood."

Bells were ringing again, this time in David's nervous system. To begin with, it was usually David who rang up Kurt, not the other way around. Kurt's calls tended to come in the dead drunk of night, his sentimental streak prompted by alcohol or any other substance that was handy. Just-ended affairs were a favorite topic, followed in both frequency and importance by buddyhood and whether or not the three surviving Beatles would ever get back together. Once he had even talked David into getting a bottle out of the cabinet and joining him in a "satellite link drink to never-ending partnership and the *White Album*." Next morning, David didn't know whom to blame the most for his hangover, Kurt or New York Telephone. Even more intriguing was the fact that Kurt was being cagy about something important enough to merit a Saturday-morning phone call. Beyond all that, Kurt was doing something he had never done before: he was asking for David's advice.

"What if I come out there?"

"Fine," Kurt answered, no doubt thinking that David was pulling his leg. "But it's an awful long way to come for the weekend."

"It wouldn't be just for the weekend. I'm due for a couple of weeks off, starting Monday."

"That's great, but don't you and your Significant Other have plans?"

"That was before I tried to actually get her on the plane. She canceled on me again. I couldn't fucking believe it. She actually suggested I go alone. Pretty romantic, eh?"

"Sounds like you just got kicked off Fantasy Island," Kurt observed grimly.

David gazed at his clothes strewn across the room and took a deep breath. His mind was a jumble. The idea of going out West to blow off a little steam with the excuse of helping an old friend certainly appealed to him. But even though he was still angry at Andrea, leaving town now would only make things worse when he got back. Besides, what if he got all the way out there and she changed her mind?

"I guess I should probably stay here and try to patch things up," he said, trying to find a graceful way to renege on his offer.

"No, hold on a minute, pal," Kurt interrupted. "The way I see it, you have absolutely no choice in the matter."

"I don't?"

"Not in the least."

"Why not?"

"For the following three reasons: one, you have a couple of weeks of unplanned time thrust into your hands, so to speak. Two, the swallows are leaving Capistrano."

"What's the third reason?"

"I need you."

"Kurt, I didn't know you cared," David retorted, trying to josh away his unease.

"Mocking me will only delay the inevitable."

"What the hell am I supposed to do in California that I can't do any number of other places?"

"Get drunk, dude," Kurt said, doing a fairly credible surf bum. "Hang ten. Get a tan. A better one, anyway. Eat decent Mexican food for a change."

A few seconds of stifled laughter.

"David, listen to me. Despite the sophomoric trimmings, this is an earnest business proposition of public importance and personal trust." There was an urgency in Kurt's tone that David would not have believed possible. "Consider it an overdue reunion between two friends who might have something more than good memories to offer each other. Just come here and hear me out. That's all I ask. If you're still not interested, I'll put you on the next plane back to New York. Either way, you get a much-needed break from the anthill. No strings, no obligation, with a money-back guarantee!"

David was dumbstruck.

"Imagine, Mr. Loya, two glorious weeks in sunny Southern California at the luxurious Randall Inn!" Kurt was now doing his sardonic game-show-host impression, but a moment ago he had been deadly serious, almost desperate. "What's it going to be, Mr. Loya? Are you going to keep what you've got—and God knows it isn't much just now—or trade everything away for what's behind door number one, where the lovely Carol Merrill is standing?"

It was still there, just beneath the flip banter. The connection. David was coming under Randall's spell all over again, just like in the old days, when they would go hunting for girls in Cambridge together and end up closing every bar in town. It was as if the years since graduation hadn't existed, as if they had not gone their own separate ways: David to do his people's counsel stint before signing up at Metcalf & Stuart, Kurt to drift through Europe and Asia until unexpectedly returning to California to run his father's re-election campaign for state senator. Since then, David had gradually begun to lose touch with his friend. He had come to accept that their closeness was not immutable, as it had once seemed, but inexorably linked to their mutual past, the product of a specific time and place, as removed from the vicissitudes of ordinary reality as student life itself.

On the rarefied streets of Cambridge they had made a striking pair: David, the swarthy newcomer, finding himself increasingly accepted and comfortable among the imposing brick buildings and tree-lined streets, and Kurt, blond and organically at ease, the liberal politician's son, constantly striving to downplay his own all-American background. There was no situation Kurt couldn't conquer, no person he couldn't win over. David had perceived something almost noble about the need to be liked in a person so apparently self-sufficient. Right from the start, Kurt had gone out of his way to befriend David, introducing him to the insulated world of *The Harvard Lampoon* and the Porcellian, showing him the ropes, even giving him tips on the carefully cultivated sloppiness of proper preppy attire. David was an exotic novelty, the savage savant fresh from the jungles of the barrio. Kurt, in turn, was David's white-bread Don Juan, instructing him in the strange but fascinating rituals of the Yankee Way of Knowledge. In time, David had come to appreciate the appeal of his own quiet charm and dark good looks enough to see that Kurt's motives were not entirely altruistic. It made sense that Kurt, who was born on the inside track and strove to get out, and David, who was born on the outside and strove to get in, would become allies. Kurt gave David credibility; David gave Kurt humanity. It became a sort of standing joke between them—who benefited more from being in the other's company. And even now, he still wasn't sure who had gotten the better part of the bargain.

"Carol Merrill is waiting," Kurt said.

2

It wasn't until his first trip home from Harvard that David got a chance to see Los Angeles from the air. He had flown into LAX many times since then, but there was still nothing stranger to him than the sight of his hometown from an overhead perspective. Even on a limpid day like this, when hot Santa Anas had scrubbed the basin free of smog, he was shocked by the city's amoebic lack of definition. Looking down, he traced the sprawling surface of cellular green lots and pulsing arteries and noticed again how much the city resembled an organism without an outer parameter or skin.

Lately, David had begun to think there was something equally amorphous about the lives of Los Angelenos. L.A., unlike New York, did not make hard bargains with its inhabitants; its allure was diaphanous and indirect, as subtle and slow as the steady seepage of carbon dioxide into the atmosphere.

Ladies and gentlemen, on behalf of our captain and the whole flight crew, I'd like to welcome you to the Los Angeles metropolitan area. The local forecast is calling for sunny skies, with a high of 82 degrees . . .

A smattering of applause rippled through the cabin.

El-Lay. The Big Orange. La Ciudad de La Virgen de los Angeles. Car Country. Shopping Mall Country. Back-yard Bar-B-Q Country. Where car exhaust fumes freely mingled

30

with the sweet smell of freshly clipped grass. Dichondra and diaspora.

The plane banked and David caught a glimpse of the Malibu shoreline, white against the brown foothills like a strip of pale flesh peeking from beneath a bikini. David was familiar with the upscale pleasures of the southland. His West Coast colleagues had welcomed him into their sunken living rooms, escorted him to Spago, Le Dome, and the West Beach Café, plied him with Simi Reserve, Courvoisier, and the finest sin semillan before a nude dip in their Jacuzzis. "You've got to be crazy to live in New York," they would say, trying to mask their defensiveness. L.A. was the mecca of the good life, the promised land, or so they never failed to remind him.

But the difference between David and his L.A. friends was that he knew there was another Los Angeles: the one he had left behind. In some ways it was farther away from the rest of the city than New York was from California. This other L.A. was where his parents were, along with the few members of his family that had not scattered to the instant suburbs blooming on the outer reaches of Orange County. Ernesto and Susanna Loya still lived in the same stucco house they had bought some thirty years ago, just before David was born. At this very moment they were probably in the midst of their Saturday-afternoon ritual. His father would be in the living room, buried in the sports pages of the newspaper; his mother in the kitchen fussing over a batch of chile verde, rushing back and forth between the stove and the television to keep track of her Spanish soaps. In the middle of supper, someone would call with news of a distant cousin and his father would yell at his mother to get off the phone and serve him. They would talk about the neighbors and the weather and how it was time to hire that old gabacho on Hubbard Street to put on a new roof before the whole thing came down on their heads like it did to poor Carlota Mendoza during the last big rain, can you imagine, God forbid. They would speak of these things in a modified form of Spanish peppered with Americanisms and old sayings, until it sounded to David like a personal code of communication. Unadulterated English was reserved for work, dealings with Anglos, and talking with their son.

The family history had always been murky. The bits and pieces that David had gleaned from his mother and grandmother were like sections of an unfinished puzzle. His maternal grandmother was a waitress in Albuquerque when William Daniels, a young roustabout who had emigrated from London's West End, stayed for three helpings of dessert before deciding that he couldn't live another day without being married to her. Lola Martínez was a savvy young woman who should have known better than to fall for a man like Bill. But, apparently, his Cockney rendition of "Las mañanitas" was more than she could resist. Lola and Bill moved to El Paso, where an aquaintance had offered him a chance to bartend in a saloon, and stayed long enough to have first Rosa and then Susanna, David's mother. Wild Bill, as he liked to be known, had met his match in Lola. Her fierce Indian pride was the equal of any man's temper, and Bill had learned it was better to stay out all night than to come home drunk and face the wrath of a woman whose father had died fighting at the side of Pancho Villa.

The girls were still in diapers when Bill and Lola up and moved to Los Angeles. The rumor that Bill had been on the run from the El Paso Police was directly contradicted by the story that maintained they had come West because Lola had dreamed of meeting Errol Flynn, which was in turn negated by a third version that held that Wild Bill and his friends were so drunk one night that they had burned the house down. Whatever the truth, the fledgling family had settled in a red-shingle bungalow in Echo Park, not far from the railroad yards where Bill managed to land a job as an assistant switchman. By the time Susanna and Rosa were old enough for school, Bill had long since jumped on the Union Pacific with a one-way ticket to God-knows-where in his hand. In retrospect, what amazed David was not that Wild Bill had left but that he had stayed so long as he had. Los Angeles in the 1930s must have seemed like a pretty small town to a man who had played in the Grand Ole Opry. As a boy, David often imagined him swinging from the side of a boxcar with a bottle of bourbon in his hand, wind whipping his mustache across ruddy cheeks as he warbled "Las mañanitas," and had vowed someday to follow in his tracks.

After Wild Bill's departure, Lola became obsessed with finding the means to provide a proper future for her daughters. She kept her husband's name and dated only wealthy men. Potential suitors were quizzed extensively about their financial resources. Far from being put off, a number of them were enticed by her combination of physical beauty and fiscal hardheadedness. In the end, Lola married none of her paramours. Instead, she borrowed enough money from them to begin her own sewing business. Like Lola herself, the designs were both attractive and practical. The business thrived, and before long she was able to buy her own house and send the girls to parochial school. When Rosa and Susanna had both been married off, Lola sold the business and retreated to her property in Echo Park. In her later years she became something of a recluse, known throughout the neighborhood for her tendency to grind her teeth and an almost unnatural devotion to reruns of *The Beverly Hillbillies*.

It was a constant source of wonder for David to realize that Lola's father could very well have been riding with the same outlaw army that had driven his paternal grandparents off their hacienda on the parched plains of Sonora. On the few occasions when both sides of the family came together, he had noticed the guarded formality with which they treated each other. Even on holidays, there was a chasm of silence that divided the Loyas and the Martínez-Daniels, like an unspoken truce between two opposing camps forced to occupy the same territory.

Having barely survived the Mexican civil war, Juan and

33

María Loya had emerged from the chaos only to discover that the deed to the family ranch, which had been craftily sewn into the hem of Doña María's skirt, was considered worthless by the new Mexican government. Penniless and physically exhausted, they had headed north to California. The ousted patriarch never recovered from the shock of losing both his country and the family fortune to the revolution. Despite his financial straits, he refused to take a "common job" and spent the remainder of his life punishing himself in bars and whorehouses. Instead of inheriting a splendid ranch, his American-born son, Ernesto, was handed a legacy of irretrievable loss. Like many other Mexicans of his generation, Juan considered "Chicano" to be a dirty word reserved for pachucos, campesinos, and other scum. Only María Loya emerged from their ordeal relatively unscathed, turning to religion and the private paradise of her garden in El Monte for the strength to accept her unlucky life. Faced with the task of supporting her husband and their new son, María worked as a salesclerk at Sears and took babysitting jobs on weekends. When the war started, Ernesto joined the Navy, but continued to help support his parents. Once a month, María would get a letter from Okinawa or Wake Island, along with a money order bought with half of his G.I. paycheck.

After V-J day, Ernesto was shipped back to L.A. The night Susanna met him at a USO gala at the Palladium, she thought he looked like Clark Gable with his uniform and pencil-thin mustache. He thought she was the spitting image of Rita Hayworth. They danced under a spinning glitter ball to the Tommy Dorsey Orchestra, and Susanna could feel herself being physically swept up in the arms of history. Ernesto courted her respectfully, cautiously, doggedly, doing everything in his power to ingratiate himself with the mercurial Lola. For her part, Susanna was attracted to his aristocratic background and his decency, two things she had always believed to be mutually exclusive. And when she found out about the checks he sent home to his mother, she made up her mind to marry him. At least I know that he'll never leave me, she reasoned. The ceremony was small and subdued by neighborhood standards, followed by a one-week honeymoon in Santa Barbara. Ernesto had become an expert welder in the Navy, and once demobilized, he landed a steady job with a construction company. A year later, they bought the house in East L.A. for $9,000 with a G.I. loan. While Ernesto never complained that the Mexican revolution and his father's incontinence had cheated him of his birthright, his resentment quietly festered as the years went by, an incurable disease destroying him from the inside. When David was born, Ernesto and Susanna realized they had been given a second chance to build a new future, and vowed to raise him with every advantage and opportunity that they had never been given.

David had learned most of what he knew about his origins from either Susanna or "Mami," his name for Grandma María. Their stories of life in Mexico seemed too fantastic to be real, as if the characters and events described were not from another country but from another planet. His father's refusal to talk about the past never bothered him until he was in high school and someone asked him exactly what part of Mexico his family was from. At that moment David realized he didn't know.

Though his work had brought him back to Los Angeles a number of times, David had gone to see his parents only twice in the past six years. It was always the same scenario: While his mother questioned him excitedly about his life in New York, his job, his latest vacation in the Caribbean, his father would watch in wordless disapproval. "So what do you do out there besides spend money?" Ernesto had blurted out once, to which Susanna had replied, "Would you be happier if he had stayed here to be a welder like you?" But his mother's words could not repair the damage. David knew that as proud as his parents were of him, he could never repay his debt as a son from so far away, and that by fulfilling their dreams for his success in a world they could never know or enter, he had simultaneously betrayed them.

The plane began its descent.

David heard a woman's voice ask, "Why aren't there any people in the swimming pools?"

Kurt was waiting for him at the gate, his nose buried in a copy of the *Congressional Quarterly*. Although David hadn't seen his old friend for over a year, there was no mistaking the athletic slouch and designer sport coat, faded jeans, and cowboy boots.

"Good cover, Comrade," Kurt said from behind the pages, "the Americanskis will never suspect a thing." He lowered the thick volume, revealing the familiar Randall grin.

"Shade," he said in greeting, invoking the old sobriquet.

"Flash," David replied. "What's up?"

The two men started to shake hands, made a clumsy attempt to hug, and ended up gripping each other's elbows.

"Let's have a look at you," David said, intentionally overdoing it. "My, how you've grown!"

"You'd be surprised," Kurt said, taking David's bag. "We've got a lot to catch up on."

They passed through a set of sliding glass doors and David was enveloped by a blast of arid heat. He could almost smell the desert. "I should have brought my safari shorts."

"You can borrow mine. They're standard issue out here." Kurt led him to a gleaming black BMW and opened the door.

"Are these standard issue, too?"

"Absolutely," Kurt affirmed, slapping the hood. "Like it?"

"I liked the old one better."

"We all have to grow up sometime, pal."

"Do we?"

Kurt climbed into the driver's seat.

36

"I'm sorry," David said after he had closed his door, "I didn't mean it to sound that way."

"No, you're right. I liked the old one better, too, but it kept breaking down on me. I'll tell you something, though. When the time finally came, I couldn't stand to trade it in. Couldn't stomach the idea of some grease monkey getting his hands all over her, touching her parts."

"So what did you do, bury her?"

"Not exactly. I torched her in an empty lot on Van Nuys, an automotive cremation of sorts. I sat there drinking a bottle of Jack Daniel's and watched her burn, remembering all the wild times we had in that old Krautmobile. Covered a few miles together. And, you know, just before the tires melted there was this explosion and I could swear I saw its little car soul emerge, rising up through the sunroof in a puff of white smoke, and drift away to the big parking lot in the sky."

"You know, Kurt, I realize now that no matter what happens, one thing will never change."

"What's that?" Kurt asked as he started the engine.

"You'll always be full of shit."

Kurt tried to look wounded, then started to laugh. They laughed together. The tension passed.

Kurt put the car in gear and accelerated, leaning over in the same motion to place a compact disc in the stereo. Twenty minutes later, they were cutting through the split-level hills of West L.A. David marveled for the hundredth time at his friend's way with an automobile. For Kurt Randall, driving was much more than an expedient way to get from point A to point B. It was about courage and speed, a litmus test of personal character. The attitude led on occasion to a certain indifference toward red lights and double lines, not to mention parking laws.

"Are you going to tell me now, or keep me in suspense for the rest of my life?" David's question ended up sounding more like a statement.

"You mean why we always have so much fun?" The grin.

"You know what I'm talking about. What is it that you needed my advice for?"

"All in good time, my friend. Relax. You just got here, remember."

"Okay. When then?"

"After dinner with my parents."

"What do your parents have to do with this?"

Kurt's eyes stayed on the road, but his grin had disappeared. "Stop being so goddamned suspicious," he said.

The Randalls lived on the summit of a sloping green hill that, unlike the surrounding estates, was unobstructed by six-foot hedges. The house itself was low and rambling, with wide bay windows that looked out over the less affluent section of Beverly Hills. Kurt dismissed it as an "expensive tract house," which David supposed was close enough to the truth, but it was still hard for him to imagine actually growing up in such an environment. As they mounted the gravel path to the front door, David noticed a brown-skinned gardener hunched over one of the flower beds. David smiled, and the man nodded back without altering his blank expression. Pushing the unlocked door open, Kurt led the way into the flagstone entry hall and bellowed, "Strike up the band, bring out the dancing girls. The prodigal son has returned!" David heard a voice coming from the kitchen, and a moment later Ann Randall emerged, an indulgent half smile playing on her mouth. A small, wiry woman, she still had the same perfect teeth and posture. David watched as she balanced on the toes of her high heels to give her son a peck on the cheek.

"You remember David, Mother," Kurt said, turning to his guest.

"Of course I do." She extended her tiny hand. "So good to see you again."

"Mother, David is joining us for dinner tonight."

"Oh? You might have given me a little advance warning, dear."

"It was sort of spur-of-the-moment."

"Well, no matter. God knows there are plates enough in this big old house." She laughed at her own joke. "Well, dinner is at seven. I hope you like lamb, David. You boys just make yourselves at home."

"Mother, this *is* my home," Kurt said dryly.

"Oh, you!" She pretended to sock Kurt with a miniature fist. "Your father will be home soon. Now, if you boys will excuse me, I've got a few more things to do." They could hear her giving orders as her heels echoed down the hallway. "Lourdes, otro plato para la mesa, por favor."

"Don't pay any attention to her," Kurt said when she was out of earshot. "She's practicing to be First Lady."

"Would your dad like to be President?" David asked, after they had made their way to Kurt's old room.

"Are you kidding?" Kurt pulled two beers out of the minibar, handed one to David, and took a long swig before continuing. "Every politician wants to be President. It's like the old masturbation joke: anybody who says they don't is either lying or stupid. Right now, though, he's got his hands full getting re-elected to the Senate."

David smiled at the unintentional pun. "He could lose?"

"He's got two good terms behind him and he's about fifteen percent ahead in the polls." Kurt crossed his arms and pursed his lips. "The bottom line is that we can't afford to be slack. Overconfidence is our biggest enemy."

David began to understand what Kurt had said about growing up. The political argot, the no-nonsense delivery, the perspective on his father's career were all brand-new. At school, Kurt's interest in politics had been mainly confined to anti-apartheid rallies and off-color comments during the six o'clock news. He had once gone so far as to say that all politicians, including his dad, were con artists who told the public only what it wanted to hear. Now here he was talking strategy. David was happy that Kurt had finally found something he could care about, but the thought of him joining the system was vaguely depressing. It seemed to signal the end of something irreplaceable. David wondered if this was what it felt like to grow up.

David glanced around the room, taking in the vintage stereo system, surfer posters, and neon Miller beer sign. His eyes stopped at a black-and-white photograph of Kurt and his father hanging behind the bar. "When was that?" David asked, nodding at the picture.

"I don't remember exactly. Some fund-raiser. It was the first time I ever wore a tuxedo. I must have been all of fifteen."

"I never noticed it before."

Kurt waited a beat before speaking. "Maybe because I just put it there."

A dark-haired girl appeared at the door and shyly announced that dinner was ready. When they entered the dining room, the Randalls were already seated. The Senator rose to greet them and David remembered how much shorter he was than he appeared on television. Darker than his son, he had a trim, compact build, a large innocent forehead, and pleading brown eyes that undermined the confidence of his features.

"Good to see you, David," the Senator said as they settled back into their chairs. "Kurt tells me that you've been working for a law firm in New York. Metcalf and partners, is it?"

"That's right, sir."

"Outstanding. A very reputable outfit. Your folks must be very proud of you."

"Yes, they are."

The Senator took a sip of his wine. "Ever thought about coming back home? This city is changing, maturing. We need more bright young men like you in Los Angeles."

"Like me, sir?"

Kurt and his father exchanged a glance; then the Senator's

eyes flicked back to David. "You know that I'm coming up for re-election this year, don't you?"

"I still try to keep up with what's happening in my home state, sir."

A faint smile creased the Senator's lips. "As you might know, I've led the fight in the state legislature calling for the rights of our new immigrants. The majority of whom are Hispanics, though not by any means exclusively, of course. You don't have to go any farther than Monterey Park to see the gains made by our Japanese and Korean friends. It's an emotional issue." The Senator paused. "Your parents are from Mexico, as I recall?"

"My parents were born here. My grandparents emigrated from Mexico; three of them, anyway."

"Right."

The Senator studied the rim of his glass for a moment and David had the absurd notion that he was about to ask him for his vote. He was holding something back, maybe just trying to find the right words. Why did all politicians make a fetish out of beating around the bush?

"Let me get right to the point, David," the Senator said, reading his mind. "The main argument that my political opponents use, and believe it or not, there are some people in this state who would like to see me lose . . ." The Senator stopped again and waited. For the audience to titter? For the ritual smattering of applause? This was turning out to be a full-scale performance. David could sense him winding up, like an all-star pitcher coiled at the mound.

". . . Their argument is that the flood of Mexican immigrants, all immigrants really, is a threat to society, that the majority of them end up in the barrio or in jail or on welfare. That argument is not only amoral and fundamentally un-American, it also happens to be patently untrue. And the best proof of that is young people like yourself—Hispanic professionals, Chicanos, whatever, who have made something of themselves, who are a credit to society."

David knew what the Senator meant and even agreed with him, but something in him rebelled at the thought of being fitted so neatly into a sociological category. The numbers might add up, but the equation was specious.

Kurt broke the silence. "I think Dad's just trying to say that he's proud of you, too."

"And that he wishes all Mexicans were just like me."

The Senator's ears had taken on a pinkish tinge. Kurt's eyes were fixed on his plate, but Ann Randall was looking around the table with obvious excitement. David watched her features twitch like a small agitated animal's and wondered if she were some sort of political voyeur, aroused only by the heat of argument. Perhaps that was why she had married a politician.

"Look, Senator Randall," David said, trying a more conciliatory tack. "I don't mean to sound rude or ungrateful, but people like me became part of the system a long time ago. Sure, we're respectable, all right, because we're assimilated. Some of us are even Republicans."

"David," the Senator stammered, "I didn't mean to imply for a second . . ."

"Sir, just let me finish, please." David realized that he had wanted to say this for years but had never had the nerve. "The point is that we already believe in education and careers and accumulating money for our old age. We've got a late-model car in the garage and a down payment on the American Dream. You think that giving someone like me a scholarship to an Ivy League university is the answer to discrimination? The fact is, people like me would get by just fine with or without affirmative action. We're not the problem. The problem is festering in the slums of Mexico City and parts of East L.A. It's the hungry wetback who can't even speak English that you should be worrying about. The poor, the hopeless, the ones joining gangs and robbing old ladies because they perceive the system itself, the status quo, to be their enemy. They are the ones who need your help the most and are the last to get it. Most of them never will."

"Now hold on a minute, son, just hold on." The Senator tried to regain the initiative. He leaned over, gesturing with his fork. "Without some sort of affirmative-action program you might have never gotten into Harvard, right? How can you sit there and tell me that going to a top-notch school has not changed your life for the better?"

Kurt and his mother had been relegated to the status of bystanders.

"Of course Harvard has made a difference," David said, suddenly weary of the whole discussion. "But I'm not quite sure what that's worth. If I had gone to, say, Cal State, I'd probably still live in Los Angeles, I'd certainly make less money. It's also safe to say that I would have never been invited to sit at this table. But does that really make me a better person? Not everyone would think so."

Ann Randall spoke first. "More lamb anyone?"

They drove to Kurt's apartment with the CD player cranked up at full volume, eliminating any chance of conversation. As the electrified rhythms shook his seat, David stared out the window at the stream of passing cars, glimpsing faces in a blur of disconnected motion. This was not the same city he grew up in. There was something alien in the air, an undertow of calculation beneath the laid-back surface. Kurt seemed different, too. There had been a time not so long ago when their friendship was effortless and automatic. Now every other sentence seemed laden with innuendo. Or was he just imagining the whole thing, a victim of self-fulfilling prophecy? Maybe Kurt and L.A. hadn't changed. Maybe it was him.

"That was quite a performance you put on during dinner," Kurt said.

"I'm sorry. Really. I hope I didn't offend your father too much."

They were standing on the deck of Kurt's beachfront condo. Ocean and sky had dissolved into a flat zone of dark purple divided by a broken chain of lights on the horizon. The churning surf was answered now and then by the whoosh of traffic on Pacific Coast Highway.

"I doubt it; disagreement stimulates him. He gets off on it. I just hope you realize he does mean well. He really is trying to help, you know."

"Sure." David's patience had just about run out. "Look, Kurt, no offense, but I didn't come out here to discuss politics with your father."

"No, I guess you didn't." Kurt had a pair of cold Coronas balanced on the railing. He opened one and held it out. When David shook his head, Kurt shrugged and took a swig himself. "About a month ago, one of my parents' maids, a girl named Josefina, decided to quit. She didn't wait around for her last check, didn't say goodbye. To tell you the truth, this sort of thing happens all the time, so nobody thought twice about it."

Kurt shuddered. "It's getting nippy out here. Let's go in."

He slid the glass door shut and motioned David to the living room.

David registered the post-dorm generic decor. "Nice place."

"Thanks." But Kurt's mind was on his story, which he told slowly, deliberately, as if he were describing the plot of a movie he'd seen.

"So, anyway, a couple of weeks ago, my dad gets a phone call from some guy named Huero, says he's the leader of some pachuco gang in East L.A. called the M-1 boys. Ever heard of them?"

"Can't say that I have."

"He says Josefina, our former employee, is with him and that she's got some papers, some papers that could be damaging to my father's re-election campaign if they got into the wrong hands. My dad just laughs and hangs up. Then he goes up to his study to look for the papers in question. He opens the locked drawer, and bingo—they're missing."

David was watching himself in the same movie, except that a different scene was playing now. He was back at the dinner table, watching Kurt's mother fidget with her food, wondering what sort of person lived inside that nervous exterior. Even the broccoli soufflé had been molded into a perfect little wedge.

Kurt was waiting for him to say something.

"What kind of papers were they?"

"Our whole media campaign strategy. How much we have, how much we're planning to spend on radio, TV, newspapers. That sort of thing."

Suddenly thirsty, David reached for the beer and took a long drink. "I don't get it. Why would he go after your dad and not the GOP?"

"It seems this Huero has something of a Benito Juárez complex. His whole rap was pretty incoherent, but I got something about him wanting my dad to add something to the election platform, the usual stuff about better housing, more schools, higher welfare payments. The guy's obviously off the wall."

"So why doesn't your father just go to the police?"

"No way." Kurt shook his head in slow motion. "We might as well send a press release to the *Times*. The media would eat it up. It would play right into the other side's hands. Our strategy would be blown and we'd look like fools to boot. This has to be dealt with as quietly as possible. Or else . . ." Kurt flopped down into a chair without finishing the sentence.

"I get the picture: Mexican Robin Hood Turns Barrio into Sherwood Forest. Film at eleven."

"Yeah. Hilarious." Kurt was staring at the carpet.

"I'm sorry," David said. "I know this is serious, but the whole thing is just so unreal. It's like some kind of TV movie of the week."

The floor vibrated slightly from the crash of a big wave or a passing truck. David wished that there was something he could do besides crack lame jokes. No wonder Kurt had been

45

edgy. Instinctively, David stood up and started to pace as he summed up the facts.

"Look, I'm no expert in criminal law," he began, "but if this is blackmail, you're dealing with real amateurs. Does your father have any enemies other than the obvious competition, people who might want to hurt him, pull a hoax?"

"My dad is a politician," Kurt said with exasperation. "By definition, half the people in this state hate his guts."

"Point taken. But if one of your dad's opponents is behind this, why didn't they just leak it to the press themselves? The same goes for the girl. Has she tried to get in touch with you herself?"

"Nope. The Huero guy says that she's too scared of getting busted by the immigration police. He says she asked him to be her spokesman."

"Tell me more about this Josefina."

"Young. Pretty. Shy."

"Did she ever do anything to tip you off? Ever catch her stealing or anything?"

"No. But then I'm not around there that much. All I know is that nobody saw it coming."

"One thing I can't understand is how your dad could be dumb enough to hire an illegal alien in the first place."

David thought Kurt was going to get angry again. But he just shrugged. "We had no idea. That new law didn't even exist when my mother hired her. Don't think the irony of the situation is lost on me. It just makes the whole mess that much more embarrassing."

For the first time that day, Kurt seemed genuinely upset. David felt sorry for his friend, but he also felt oddly exhilarated. Kurt was, in effect, asking for his professional advice.

"I think it's a bluff," he announced.

Kurt's mood instantly brightened. "So do I. The trouble is how to call their hand. There has to be a way to head those bastards off."

"The first step would be to find this Josefina and get her side of the story."

46

"Elementary, Watson."

"So why don't you sic some of your dad's people on it?"

Kurt shook his head again. "Too touchy. What we don't need is for this to come off like some kind of Watergate cover-up. It has to be someone from the outside who won't attract too much attention. Someone totally trustworthy. Chicano, ideally."

The floor vibrated again.

"Tide's coming in," Kurt said matter-of-factly.

David almost laughed aloud. He had walked right into it, set himself up. The palms of his hands felt clammy; from this angle, the office intrigues of New York seemed invitingly direct and predictable.

"You mean someone like me," David said.

"I always said you were the smartest cabrón I ever met."

So that was the catch. In college wrestling it was called a reversal. The player on the bottom flips his opponent over, thus gaining the advantage. It was worth two points. David had never liked the claustrophobic sensation of being pinned down, and he didn't like it now.

"Don't you mean the dumbest?"

It was Kurt's turn to act surprised.

"Is that why you took me over to your parents' tonight?" David asked. "So that your dad could give me his little pep talk?"

"He doesn't know anything about this. Believe me, he'd freak out if he knew that I'd told you."

"Why don't you try that one on your gardener, Kurt?"

"Hey, don't give me that pseudo-racist bullshit. We're best friends for life, remember? Butch and Sundance."

"How about Tonto and the Lone Ranger?" David turned to get Kurt's reaction. The irony was drained from the blue eyes, replaced by something that made David even more afraid.

"What about that stirring little speech you made tonight?" Kurt said sarcastically. "Didn't you mean any of it, or was that just to hear yourself talk? Blowing off a little yuppie guilt, amigo? Here's a chance to actually do something, to try to help one of those people you spoke so compassionately about."

When Kurt spoke again his voice was almost gentle. "Just help me find the girl, that's all. You know East L.A. It's your old turf. I'm asking you as a friend. You don't even have to speak to her. Just find out where she is and I'll do the rest."

David said nothing. He felt completely irresolute. Had his talk at dinner been so much feckless philosophizing, the self-righteous ranting of a guilty conscience?

. . . the sybarites of Saks, the vermin of Bloomingdale's . . .

"Besides, you owe me one," Kurt said.

"What do you mean?"

"Cape Cod."

"That was totally different."

"Do this for me and we'll be even."

David started to say something, then changed his mind.

"Just sleep on it," Kurt said. "We'll talk in the morning."

Kurt shut his bedroom door and David sat motionless for a while on the black leather sofa. All he could think about was what Kurt had said about the Cape. It seemed such a long time ago. He had a sudden urge to go for a walk. Maybe some fresh air would help clear his mind. He picked up his jacket and quietly let himself out the front door. No need to tell Kurt; he would be gone for just a few minutes. There were only two possible ways to go, along the sandy shoulder of PCH or turn left down a small side street. The side street seemed a lot safer, considering the speed of the passing traffic. Besides, wasn't this an exclusive neighborhood? David turned his collar up against the stiff ocean breeze and started walking. He knew already that he would do what Kurt wanted, against his better instincts, as he had so many times before. Like when they traipsed off for a week in Canada on a bet, or the time they had taken each other's ethics final. But they weren't college kids anymore and this wasn't spring break. The stakes were higher, and David could feel himself tottering as certainties sifted away like sand beneath him. The power to control his own life was slipping out of his hands, which was probably why he had ended up back in California in the first place. Now, by bad luck or fateful design, he was closing the circle of his past without knowing which point would lead him to the focus.

A car turned down the street behind him. David waited for it to pass. When it didn't he turned around, half expecting it to be Kurt. The light caught him full in the face, blinding him. He could hear the police radio crackling from inside the patrol car. David shielded his eyes with his hand and took a step forward.

"Can I help you, Officer?"

"Just stay where you are," the cop ordered, keeping the light on him.

"Is that spotlight necessary, Officer?" David could feel his heart pumping. The light moved closer; boots crunched on gravel.

"May I see some identification, please?"

"Why, am I suspect or something?"

"Just cut the lip and show me some I.D." The cop was classic LAPD—a redneck bureaucrat with a license to kill.

"This says you live in New York, mister. What brings you to this particular street at this time of night?"

David remembered a Ray Bradbury story called "The Pedestrian." He hoped this encounter didn't have the same ending.

"I'm staying with a friend of mine. It's not illegal to walk around after dark, is it?" David knew it was pointless to argue, but he couldn't keep an edge of sarcasm out of his response.

"What's his address?"

"I don't remember. It's just around the corner on PCH. Besides, if you could read, you would have noticed that there's also an L.A. address on my license."

"Look, Loya, I'm not sure what you're doing sneaking

around in a nice neighborhood like this, but if you want to talk smart, I'll be happy to continue this chat down at the station house."

David considered his options, feeling the heat of the engine on his Reeboks. He came to a decision. But he had to clench his teeth to say it.

"No, sir."

"I'm happy to hear that," the cop said. "Now I suggest you head back to your friend's house before you get lost or something."

Kurt had already turned in for the night when David got back to the apartment. He locked the door behind him and immediately reached for the phone. After four rings the answering machine picked up and he heard Andrea's voice say she would be away on business for a few days, followed by a beep.

"I liked the old message better," David said.

3

The midmorning traffic on the Santa Monica Freeway was still bumper to bumper as David cautiously merged into the passing lane heading east. He was gradually readjusting to the horizontal life-style. After spending so much time in New York taxis, he found driving a novelty, and he enjoyed the way the rental responded to the swift kick of octane.

A bottle blonde in a faded blue Camaro pulled abreast of him and glanced over. Keeping one eye on the road, David glanced back and smiled, instinctively adhering to the unwritten rules of highway courtship. She was singing along with her radio, her head rocking back and forth to the rhythm like a sinner at a gospel meeting. David turned on his own radio, hoping to tune in to her wavelength. He scanned the dial, catching fragments of Top 40 rock, cola theme songs, and deejay voices, searching in vain for the elusive frequency. He had read someplace about a singles club that communicated by way of coded bumper stickers. If a member spotted an appealing prospect cruising down Melrose, they could call a central computer and a meeting would be arranged at the nearest service station. Drive-through romance. Free parking.

Just beyond the San Diego interchange the road opened up and the Camaro pulled away in a plume of blue-black exhaust. As if by agreement, the rest of the cars picked up the pace.

David inhaled and knew again what it was like to live on these roads, to get a legal high on the industrial aroma of gasoline and burning rubber. He pulled off his shirt with one hand and rolled down the window, letting the warm air buffet his chest and face. The car moved with the flow of traffic, weaving and braking in a choreographed dance of metal and glass. The speedometer read 70, but there was no chance of slowing down without causing an accident. Someone had told him once about a friend of theirs getting a ticket for going five miles an hour below the legal speed limit. The officer had explained that refusing to speed along with everyone else could be considered reckless driving.

Like common sense, time and space became distorted; the faster David went, the more things around him appeared to be moving in slow motion. He glided past a rusty pickup truck with a couch hanging from the tailgate, an elderly woman in a black Jaguar, a teenager in a perfectly preserved VW bug. It occurred to David that automobiles represented the quintessential contradiction of post-industrial democracy: individualized mass movement. The drivers were at once alone and together, united and synchronized by their common velocity and direction. It was as if they were riding a single hurling ribbon of tar and concrete, a sweeping asphalt rapids. David pressed down again on the accelerator. There was no turning back, no stopping.

. . . ROBERTSON . . . LA CIENEGA . . . WASHINGTON . . .

The signs began as specks above the dashboard, bloomed ominously in the windshield, and flickered overhead before reappearing in the rearview mirror. Twenty minutes later he passed the small cluster of skyscrapers that marked the center of town and crossed over the perpetually parched bed of the Los Angeles River. Then he switched over to the Pomona Freeway, letting it guide him into the variegated landscape of East L.A.

. . . LORENA . . . INDIANA . . . DOWNEY . . .

David eased up on the gas, allowing wind and gravity

to take their revenge as he coasted toward the Atlantic
Boulevard off ramp. Bearing left, he skirted Montebello
and Monterey Park, snaking past the Pep Boys auto supply
and Safeway supermarket where, on certain nights, the
same part of Atlantic became a drag strip straightaway. Then,
just before Whittier, he took another right, entering a grid
of tree-lined side streets. He had no trouble finding the address Kurt had given him; the faces were different but the
neighborhood itself was unchanged. He drove slowly past
the nondescript houses, looking for the slightest trace of his
having grown up there, waiting for the wave of nostalgia that
never came.

Josefina had lived in a Spanish-style bungalow hemmed
in by cracked sidewalks and a peeling white picket fence.
The unkempt lawn was a graveyard for discarded toys—a
crippled wagon, a dismembered doll, a scattered platoon of
soldiers, a torn baseball card.

David approached the screen door and knocked. From a
porch across the street, an old woman watched him with
attention as she slowly fanned herself. Farther up the block,
combat-garbed preteens mounted an armed assault on their
friends. David waited a while, knocked again. Somewhere
in the back-yard maze of chain-link barricades, two unseen
dogs barked at each other. David could smell hair spray and
boiling beans. He heard a refrigerator door slam, then heavy
footsteps.

"Bueno?" A rotund woman in a red polka-dot dress was
appraising him through the fine wire mesh. "Jez, mister?"

"Buenos días, señora," David said. "I'm looking for Josefina Juárez."

The woman puckered her fat cheeks. "She no here. Se fue.
She's gone."

"That's what I understand. Could I just talk with you for
a minute?"

"I'm sorry, mister. I don't know nothing."

She started to close the door.

"Por favor," David blurted. "Soy familia de Josefina."

The woman held the door, her curiosity piqued. "Hermano?"

"Sobrino. Her cousin. Did Josefina live with you?"

The woman wiped her plump fingers on her apron. "Atrás." She motioned toward the back yard.

"Could you show me, please? Es muy importante."

"Hablas español?" she asked, still suspicious of her well-dressed visitor.

"Sí, un poco. Soy chicano. Entiendo todo, but I don't speak it so well. I understand everything, though." Which was true, despite his lousy accent.

"Quién va a pagar la renta? Me debe por este mes."

"How much did she owe you?"

"Fifty."

David pulled two twenties and a ten from his wallet.

"You'll show me her apartment?" David asked before handing her the cash.

"Sí, como no." The woman took the money and disappeared into the house, returning after a moment with a set of keys dangling from her hand.

"Venga," she ordered. "Follow me."

Outside in the blunt heat of day she seemed to relax a little, and her English improved dramatically. David learned that her name was Lupe Sánchez and that she had rented the room over her garage to Josefina for the better part of a year. With a little prompting, Doña Sánchez began to talk.

"She was, you know, pretty and shy and didn't bother nobody for nothing. Sometimes I feel sorry for her and I take her a plate of tamales. On días de fiesta I take her my special tamales."

"You must be quite a good cook." Doña Sánchez was clearly flattered.

"You come back and I give you some," she exclaimed with a generous wave of her arm. "The best in the neighborhood! I learned how to make them when I was a little girl in Jalisco. You live in Los Angeles?"

"New York."

"I knew she had familia in Mexico, but she never said nothing about a cousin in New York."

"Did she have any boyfriends?" David asked, changing the subject.

"I told her right away: You want to bring men to your bed, you go to a hotel. But," Doña Sánchez let a blast of air through her lips, "she never did nothing like that. I don't think so, anyway. I mean, quién sabe. You can't watch somebody all night, eh?"

"When did she move out?"

"About, let me see, two weeks ago, más o menos. Ha desaparecido. She was here one minute and bye-bye the next minute. Just like that. Poof! Not even saying thank you or paying the last rent, that's why I ask you, because you are her cousin. Watch your feet, please. These steps are all podridos and I don't want to go to court for your broken neck! Today, everybody sues everybody. Latinos against Latinos, gringos against gringos. Hijos sue their own mothers. That's gratitude for you, even after taking her in off the street like a lost cat. Now I need somebody to take her place, and that's not so easy, I tell you."

David nodded sympathetically as she led him up the stairs.

"I mean, you have to ask a fortune for a security deposit just to sleep in peace at night, you know what I mean?" Doña Sánchez paused to catch her breath. "Josefina is in some kind of trouble? No? I'm just asking because a gringo was here asking questions the other day. But don't worry, I act like I don't speak English. It's funny. Those gringos are so dumb they believe anything. At first I'm afraid you are him again or police or, Dios mío"—Doña Sánchez crossed herself—"from the immigration—la migra. You never know. Pueden show up at the house or the job wanting to see the green cards. Papeles. Show me your papers, they tell them, and then they take them away. Sometime the people, they come back, como nada. So I'm keeping Josefina's room empty for the rest of the month in case she comes back, too. God willing. My Lord, these stairs get higher cada año. I'm too old for this, pero qué hago? Estoy sola since my husband died. Not that he was so much help alive, the good-for-nothing. Josefina was the best renter I ever had. Una mujer santa. You know, she was a saint, that girl."

With a dramatic wheeze, Doña Sánchez hauled herself up onto the cramped landing. She fumbled with the keys until, grunting with satisfaction, she located the right one and turned it in the lock.

At first David thought that the room had been cleared out. But as his eyes adjusted to the indoor gloom, he began to make out a narrow bed, a chair, a chipped dresser adorned with a piece of white lace, and a crucifix on the wall over the bed. In the corner, a hot plate and a few utensils comprised the kitchen. There was no television or phone, just a small clock radio and some comic-book-style romance novellas. The closet was a small indentation separated from the rest of the room by a plastic curtain hanging on a single wire. There was a small shelf at the back of the closet, and on impulse David ran his hand along the edge, stopping when his fingers came across a small square of paper. It turned out to be a black-and-white snapshot of a young girl in a plain white dress. The background was nothing more than an overexposed building and a darker patch of sky. It could have been taken anywhere, anytime.

Doña Sánchez didn't notice David slipping the picture into his pocket.

"Have you ever heard of the M-1 boys?" David asked.

She made the sign of the cross again.

"The M-1 boys are trouble. You look like a smart boy, I bet you have a good job. You're better if you stay away from them."

"Is this part of their territory?"

"Look, I mind my own business. I don't know nothing about gangs. Muchachos malditos." Her voice trailed off in a string of muttered invectives.

"I understand. What did Josefina do on weekends? She must have had some friends or something."

Doña Sánchez put her hand on her bosom and rolled her eyes toward the ceiling. "Her friends were God and the Sisters. She went to church every Sunday and sometimes Saturdays. Muy religiosa."

"A local church?"

"Aquí." She raised her bulky arm and pointed. "La Guadalupe."

David thanked her for her trouble and descended the creaky wooden steps to the driveway. As he began walking to the car, a boy in camouflage fatigues jumped out of the bushes and pointed a plastic rifle at his heart.

"Surrender, yanqui—or die," he demanded.

David hadn't been inside a church in years. His parents, like most lapsed Catholics, had felt compelled to send their son to catechism school, in effect punishing him for their own lack of piety. The Sisters had done their best to teach him about Lucifer and the Holy Ghost, and he studied the Ten Commandments and tried to decipher the difference between a venal and a mortal sin, confessing only the former to a faceless priest, who seemed to be talking to himself behind the perforated grating. David had found it difficult to accept the concept that God could be both absolute and all-forgiving, omnipotent yet powerless—or unwilling—to prevent his creations from sinning. By the time he was ready for his confirmation, David knew that he was irredeemably agnostic. But rather than reveal his true belief—or lack of it—he continued to take the sacraments and go to church, dressed uncomfortably in his Sunday best. Better to be safe, he reasoned, than to run the risk of frying in hell.

On Christmas Eve, when the family knelt in prayer before

the crèche his grandmother lovingly assembled every year, he bowed his head along with the others and mouthed the Lord's Prayer, hardly hearing the words. Instead, David would focus his attention on the statues gleaming under tinsel and colored bulbs, letting his eyes be dazzled by the light that couldn't reach his soul.

By his junior year in college he had moved from the spiritual existentialism of Dostoevsky to Zen and the occult; he had only flirted with Marxism but had consummated an affair with a pretty astrologer who had guessed he was a Gemini at a rooftop frat party. Then, unexpectedly, in Italy the following summer, David had a genuine religious experience. He was in Rome and decided to visit St. Peter's, a trip he made more out of obligation than interest, having seen pictures of Michelangelo's masterpieces and the Pope saying Easter Mass on television all his life. As it turned out, however, he was overwhelmed by the sensation of being there in the flesh. The sublime scale of the courtyard, the exquisite beauty of the twisting gold columns and vaulted ceilings reaching up to heaven had taken his breath away. Sitting in a pew illuminated by slashing shafts of sunlight, David experienced a genuine sense of awe, brought on not by the glory of God but by the monumental evidence of man's sheer effort to transcend his own mortality. Here, amid the Baroque renderings of suffering saints and flying angels, was tangible proof of a degree of faith that David could only begin to imagine. He knew then that God was something he could understand but never know, something he could see but never touch. But far from being proud of this, David felt ashamed. And from that day on, even the plainest church stirred in him the guilt of the heretic forever doomed to remain in his own doubt.

Walking past the scuffed pews of Our Lady of Guadalupe, David tried to imagine Josefina Juárez kneeling at the altar and envied her. She had been able to find refuge here. Whereas all David could feel was the unease of the interloper whose very presence was a mockery of something sacred and un-knowable.

The rectory was located behind the church proper, next to a parking lot that, judging from the circles and diagonal lines on its surface, doubled as a playground during lunch-time. As he approached the building, David spied a man in neatly pressed slacks coming toward him.

"Excuse me, I'm looking for the pastor," David said.

"I'm a priest," the man answered curtly. "Can I help you?"

"I'm trying to locate someone. A Mexican girl. Early twen-ties, long black hair. Doesn't speak much English, if any. I was told by her landlady that she came here often."

"And what is your interest in her?" the priest asked.

"She's been missing for a couple of weeks. I'm a friend. Her employer has asked me to help find her. My name is David Loya."

David extended his hand, but the priest only nodded. David swallowed hard.

"And you are Father . . . ?"

"Rodríguez."

"Can you help me?"

Father Rodríguez looked at David as if he had just asked for a million dollars.

"Mr. Loya, you've just described about half my parish-ioners. I'd need a lot more information . . ."

"Her name is Josefina Juárez."

David took the snapshot out of his pocket and showed it to him.

"I'm sorry," Father Rodríguez said as he stared at the faded image. "Maybe Sister Ramona can help you. She makes a special effort with girls like the one you're describing. She's teaching a class in there right now. It should be over soon, if you don't mind waiting a few minutes. Now, if you'll excuse me . . ." He handed the photo back to David.

"Yes, of course. Thank you, Father."

David went inside and found himself inside a reception

59

area that looked like a cross between a classroom and a lower-middle-class living room. Overstuffed sofas alternated with stacks of textbooks and religious pamphlets. From somewhere down the hall David could hear children singing and, leading them in the hymn, a woman's voice, strong and insistent. David picked up a magazine, flipped idly through the pages, and, finding it was a year old, put it aside.

The next thing on the pile was a booklet titled *The True Story of the Apparitions of Our Lady of Guadalupe.* The cover pictured a young Indian in white peasant clothes gazing up at a woman sheathed in an aura of radiant light. Her head and shoulders were covered by a blue cowl decorated with gold stars. At her feet, an angel hovered adoringly on a cushion of clouds. He remembered seeing a similar picture on his grandmother's dresser when he was a boy and being amazed at the Virgin's ability to look simultaneously happy and sad, splendid and humble.

David opened the pamphlet and began to read the rococo typeface.

Herewith follows a carefully ordered account of the marvelous manner in which the Ever Virgin Saint Mary, Mother of God, Our Queen, called Guadalupe, recently appeared on Tepeyacac Hill, December 1531:

It was ten years after the fall of Mexico City, a time when peace blessed the countryside after many years of strife, that the Divine Lord, Author of Life, began to look once again to earth and extend his hand to the people. The first person to see the manifestation of His blessed will was a poor Indian named Juan Diego. Very early one Saturday morning, Juan Diego, who lived in Cuautitlán, was on his way to service and to do errands when he came upon the hill of Tepeyacac. It was dawn and the land was very still. Suddenly he heard singing from the top of the hill. The singing was like a million beautiful birds, only lovelier. It seemed to pour across the hillside, bathing everything in its golden sound. At first, Juan Diego thought he was dreaming. "Am I still at home in slumber," he asked himself. "Or have I died and gone to heaven?" Then the singing stopped and Juan Diego heard someone calling to him from the top of the hill, saying: "Little Juan, little Juan Diego. Come to me. Hurry. I am waiting for you."

Being pure of mind and body, Juan Diego was not the slightest bit afraid. In fact, his heart leapt with joy as he climbed the hill toward the voice that called to him. Once at the summit, he saw a beautiful lady who told him to come forward. As he came closer, Juan Diego was astounded by her superhuman magnificence. Her vestments sent forth a sun-like radiance. The rock upon which she stood was shot through with bolts of blinding light and the ground below was covered by a rainbow. The mesquite and prickly pears that grew around the rock shone like emeralds; the branches and thorns glittered like gold.

Juan Diego fell to his knees, and the Lady spoke to him in a mellifluent voice, with the manner of someone who loved him greatly. "Juanito, smallest of my children, where goest thou?"

"My Lady," he answered, "I must go to your house in Mexico Tlatiloco and continue to study the Divine Mysteries taught to us by the priests."

She spoke again, saying, "Be it known and understood by you, the smallest of my children, that I am the Ever Virgin Saint Mary, Mother of the true God from whom all life has come, and that I ardently desire a temple to be built for me, wherein I can offer and show all my love, compassion, help, and protection. For I am your merciful Mother, wishing to hear and help you and all who dwell in this land. And in order to carry out what my mercy seeks, you must go to the Bishop's palace in Mexico and tell him that I sent you to make it clear how very much I desire that he build a temple for me here on this place. You shall tell him exactly all that you have seen and marveled at and what you have heard. Be certain that I shall be very grateful and reward you," the Lady continued. "Go now, my son, the smallest of us all, and give it your best effort."

Whereupon Juan Diego bowed low before her and said, "My Lady, I am going now to carry out your command. For the present, your humble servant takes leave of you." Then he went down the hill and set out to do her bidding on the causeway that leads to Mexico.

Once inside the city, Juan Diego went straight to the palace of the Bishop, who was named Friar Don Juan de Zumarraga. Juan Diego knocked at the gates of the palace and implored the servants to announce him. And after a good while, they came to call him, for the Bishop had ordered that he enter. Juan Diego knelt before the Bishop and immediately gave him the message from the Lady of Heaven, telling him also everything he had seen and heard. After listening to everything Juan Diego had to say, the Bishop nodded but did not seem to believe him. "Thank you, my son," he said. "You shall come again and I will hear you at greater leisure. I shall look into the matter carefully and give much thought and consideration to the good will and desire with which you have come."

Juan Diego thanked him and left, but he did so sadly, for he had by no means accomplished the purpose of his errand. He returned the very same day to the top of the hill and found the Lady of Heaven, who was waiting for him at the same place. Immediately he fell to his knees and addressed her: "My Lady, I went where you sent me to carry out your order, although it was difficult for me to enter the Bishop's audience chamber. I saw him and delivered your message exactly as instructed. He received me kindly and listened with attention, but as soon as he spoke, it was clear that he did not believe me. I understand perfectly from the way he responded that he thinks I made the whole story up. So I earnestly entreat you, my Lady, to entrust one of the important people with the message, someone well known, respected, and held in high esteem. For I am but a little man and you, my Lady, send me where I am out of place and have no standing. Forgive me if I cause you much grief and make you angry with me, my Lady and Mistress."

The most Holy Virgin answered: "Listen to me, smallest of all my beloved children, and understand that my servants and messengers are many, and that any one of them can be ordered to take my message and do my bidding. But it is in every way necessary that you solicit my cause and help me, and that it be through your intercession that my wish be carried out. My little son, I urge and firmly order you to go again to the Bishop tomorrow. Tell him in my name and make him fully understand my disposition: that he start work on the temple I ask of him. Tell him again that I in person, the Ever Virgin Saint Mary, Mother of God, sent you."

Juan Diego answered: "My Lady, may I cause you no worry or trouble. I shall go very gladly as you command. Tomorrow, toward sunset, I will return and give an account of the Bishop's response. I must now go on my way." Then Juan Diego went to his house to rest.

The following day was Sunday, and in the very early dawn he dressed and left his house and went directly to Tlatiloco for religious instruction, holding in mind that he was to see the Bishop directly afterwards. He arrived just before ten o'clock, heard Mass, and, when the crowd was dispersing, set out for the Bishop's palace. As soon as he arrived, he insisted on being seen, and after many difficulties was able to get in to see the Bishop. Kneeling down before him, he repeated sadly and tearfully the order he brought from the Lady of Heaven, for he was exceedingly anxious to be believed. The Bishop, in order to verify the matter, asked him many questions. Where had he seen her? What was she like? But even though Juan Diego gave a full account of everything with great exactitude, the Bishop did not believe him and said he could not carry out the order merely on the *basis of Juan Diego's account, unless he first received a direct sign from the Blessed Virgin herself. Upon hearing the Bishop's words, Juan Diego said, "Seigneur, just what kind of sign do you ask for, for I shall go and request it from the Lady of Heaven, who sent me."*

After Juan Diego left, the Bishop had him followed by members of the household whom he could trust, so that they could watch where he went, and whom he saw and spoke to. This they did. Juan Diego walked straight ahead, taking the causeway. Those who followed lost sight of him where the road goes by the ravine near the bridge of Tepeyacac. And although they looked everywhere, there was no trace of him to be found anywhere. So they turned back unhappily, not only because he had slipped out of sight, but because his behavior had given them so much trouble. After they had told the Bishop what had happened, he was inclined to disbelieve the whole matter. For they also said that they were being deceived, that Juan Diego was making up what he had told or dreamt up the whole story, and they inferred that if he should come back he should be punished severely, so that he would never tell lies and make fools of them again . . .

Children were running down the hallway in an echoing commotion of stamping feet and chatter. David put the booklet in his pocket and moved toward the doorway where he had heard the woman's voice. She was dressed in a traditional black-and-white habit, sorting papers on a scratched oak desk. As he entered the classroom she looked up sharply, as if he were a trespasser.

"Can I help you?" she inquired.

Her hair was hidden by her wimple, but David could see that, in contrast to the homely nuns that resided in his memory, she was young and attractive.

David introduced himself and showed her the picture.

"Yes, I know her," she said in crisp English. "Her faith is

very strong. But I'm sorry to have to tell you that I haven't seen her in several weeks."

"She disappeared around that time," David said. "I thought maybe you'd have some idea of where she went."

Her hazel eyes stabbed at him again. "I have no idea. But even if I did, I wouldn't tell you."

"Why not?"

"Because you're full of bull."

"I'm sorry?" The church *had* changed.

"I don't know who you are, Mr. Loya, but you are certainly not Josefina's brother. Don't you know that lying is a sin?"

David couldn't help noticing the white tennis shoes peeking out from under her skirt.

"You're right, I'm not her brother," he admitted, chagrined that he had even tried to deceive her. David had the distinct impression that this tough-talking nun would be a valuable ally. Maybe it wasn't too late to earn her trust.

"Listen, I'm not a cop or an immigration officer. All I want to do is find out where she is and if she's okay. A friend of mine wants to talk to her, that's all."

"I'm sorry, Mr. Loya," she said, rising to dismiss him, "I have nothing more to say."

"Maybe you should reconsider," David said, "for Josefina's sake. I have reason to believe that she's mixed up with a local gang called the M-1 boys. I take it you've heard of them. It's also possible that she's been kidnapped. I'm one of the few people who might be able to help her."

Sister Ramona had begun to finger her rosary. When she spoke again it was with less hostility. "I know she was afraid someone was going to hurt her."

"Is there some way to reach her?" David asked. "Someone in her family?"

"She doesn't have any. Not here, anyway. Her father was killed when she was a little girl. Her mother died a few years later in the slums outside Mexico City. She came here stuffed with a dozen other people in the back of a truck. No food or water for twelve hours. A lot of them never survive. She was lucky, at least for a while. I found her a place to live. She worked as a housekeeper for some big politician who lives in Beverly Hills. She often came here to pray."

"There has to be a way to find her. I know she was religious; she must have trusted you. Did she ever mention any friends?"

Sister Ramona adjusted her wimple, a gesture he found charming.

"There was a girl who worked with her. Her name was Marta. But I think she was planning to go back to Mexico. I'm not sure."

"Do you know how I might get in touch with her?"

"Why don't you call her boss?"

"Good idea," David said, deciding not to give away more than he had to.

"Look, Mr. Loya, I have a lot of work to do."

"I understand. Is it all right if I check back with you in a day or two?"

"Suit yourself."

"Thanks." He watched her collecting her things. "One last question: Is there any chance she might have gone back to Mexico with her friend?"

"It's possible," Sister Ramona said hesitantly. "I do know this: wherever she is, Santa Guadalupe is with her."

"Madre de Dios! Ernesto! Come and look who's here!"

David's mother was holding the door open with one hand, the spoon she used to stir the beans clutched in the other.

"Ernesto!" she called as she hugged and kissed her son. "It's your hijo!"

His parents had grown used to him dropping in out of the blue this way. The pattern dated back to his rebellious teens,

66

when David had insisted on coming and going whenever he pleased. Funny thing was, the older he got, the more useful the privilege became.

David could hear the muted din of the television set coming from the rear of the house. Momentarily, his father emerged, squeezing his son's arm as if sizing up a welterweight contender. "Mire, Susanna, he's like skin and bones," he said, shaking his head. "Don't they feed you anything in New York?"

"I'm old enough to feed myself, Dad."

"David, mijo, come and sit," his mother ordered. "I'm making chile verde, your favorite."

They took their places at the imitation-marble Formica table, David sitting across from his father. In the adjoining family room a toddler sat sucking its thumb, transfixed by a Pepsi commercial in Spanish. David noted that, unlike opera, ads were just as inane in a different tongue.

"Who's the kid?" he inquired casually.

"Ours," his father deadpanned. "Your mother's been pregnant since the last time we saw or heard from you." The old man had not lost his knack.

"Don't talk like that," his wife scolded from the kitchen, adding for David's sake, "That's Vera's little girl, from across the street. We're babysitting while they go to the movies. They went to see that new one by the actor with the mustache."

"For a second there, I thought I had a new sister," David said, picking up on his father's joke.

"More kids," Ernesto replied incredulously. "What for? So that they can move away and desert you when they grow up?"

"Ernesto, por favor, don't start," his wife implored as she ladled the thick green sauce onto their plates. "No wonder he never comes home anymore."

David loved to watch his mother in the kitchen. When she was cooking one of her specialties, the whole universe revolved around her cluttered stove. Tall and full-figured, with henna-red hair, she was like some kind of animated bird as she chattered away, her hands flapping through clouds of steam that reeked of cilantro and maize and hot jalepeño peppers. When David was a child he used to hide under her billowing apron and imagine that she was a powerful sorceress performing flavorful feats of ancient alchemy.

"Susanna, más tortillas," Ernesto barked.

The way David's father always took his wife for granted sent a jolt of anger through him.

"Mom, when is Dad going to buy you a new dinner table, for Christ's sake?" he complained, even though he knew it was a violation of the truce. "It's not as if you don't have the money."

"I know, mijo, I'm just waiting for Vera to come with me to help pick out a nice one."

"The furniture isn't good enough for him anymore" came the inevitable challenge. "Maybe your mother and I should go out and change our clothes? Susanna, go get my tuxedo so that my son is not embarrassed."

"Dad, lay off for once. You know that's not what I meant."

"Don't argue, eat!" his mother commanded, pushing a hot tortilla into her husband's hand.

David tried not to watch as he folded the flour pancake into a shovel and scooped the food into his mouth.

"And so what brings you home, son?" his mother inquired cheerfully. "Is it work or just a social visit?"

"A little bit of both, I guess."

"Didn't you know he gets paid just to fly around and have fun?"

David and his mother ignored him.

"And New York?" Susanna continued. "You still like it there?"

"Yeah, it's fine, Mom. Just fine."

What else could he tell her? That a computer-chip company was being sued for patent infringement on a component that would never reach the market. That anyone at his firm who questioned the fee-generating logic of this was ordered to take a vacation. That there was a new discotheque in Manhattan that was popular because it was run by transvestites. That his girlfriend had become a stranger to him. That he no longer knew where he came from, or where he belonged.

Ernesto pushed his plate away and cleared his throat, the signal that he was about to make a pronouncement.

"Oh boy, here it comes," David said under his breath.

"Did you say something, hijo?"

"Not really."

"Your grandmother is getting old," Ernesto groused. "We won't have her much longer, you know."

David looked at his mother, but her eyes told him, *Don't worry, it's the same old stuff. Just humor him as you always do.*

"She's almost eighty-five," he continued, oblivious to their exchange. "It's her birthday Friday, you know."

"Don't worry, Dad. I didn't forget. I'll stop by tomorrow on my way to Johnny's house."

David pretended not to feel his father's eyes boring a hole in the side of his head.

"I thought we agreed you weren't going to hang around with those bums? Haven't you learned your lesson yet? Are you stupid or something?"

"Not Johnny, Dad." David was losing the fight to control his temper. "He's not like them. He's not in the gang anymore. He's the only one who tried to help me."

"I don't care," Ernesto said. "Remember what happened last time?"

David felt as if someone had punched him in the stomach. *If it weren't for her,* he told himself. *If it weren't for my mother . . .*

"Thanks for dinner, Mom," he said, purposely averting his eyes from his father. "I'll be in touch."

69

"Ernesto! Apologize to your son. Tell him to stay."

As he stood to leave, David couldn't help noticing that the little girl's eyes were still glued to the TV set. He looked at the screen and saw a man in a mariachi suit standing in a huge parking lot, singing a song about Ford pickups.

The Pretenders were blasting from the stereo when David got back to the apartment. He found Kurt in the kitchen, rummaging for food like a hungry bear. "Mind if I turn this down a little?"

"If it isn't the redoubtable Inspector Loya," Kurt said from inside the refrigerator. "Sure, go ahead. You're just in time for dinner."

"No thanks, I just ate," David said, grabbing a beer for himself.

"Does that mean you don't want one of my famous custom slabs on rye, or are you making a moral judgment?"

"I've never had much of an appetite for either. How's the democratic process going?"

"Not bad." Kurt took a bite and chewed thoughtfully, as if expecting the food in his mouth to tell him something. "I'm hoping to have some interesting statistics for you in a couple of days. Any news from the terrorist front?"

"She's gone, all right," David reported. "Didn't even say goodbye to her landlady. Someone else has been snooping around, too."

"Cops?"

"Doubt it. She wouldn't go to the police on her own, or to anyone else as far as I can tell. She could have been picked up by immigration, or even gone back to Mexico, but it's not likely."

"Why's that?" Kurt squeezed a lime into his beer and took a long gulp.

"One of the nuns at the church she went to said she was afraid someone was after her."

"Any idea who?"

"If she had one she wasn't saying. Do you?"

"It's a medieval tradition—Byzantine secrecy, secular subterfuge, you know." Kurt flashed an insinuating smile. "Our friends the M-1 boys maybe."

"Maybe," David allowed. "Does a girl named Marta work for your parents?"

Kurt stopped chewing. "What's she got to do with this?"

"Nothing probably. But I'd like to talk to her."

"That could be difficult. She split a couple of months ago. Thomas Wolfe was wrong. You can go home again—with enough U.S. dollars stashed away. Forget about Marta. These people are transients, most of them. You're lucky if you have time to learn their names. So what's our next move?"

"The M-1 boys," David said. "I think I know how to find them."

"You figure she's with them?"

"I'd bet my huaraches on it."

Kurt grinned and tipped his chair back until it was resting against the wall at a 45-degree angle. He stayed like that, suspended between sitting and falling, apparently digesting their conversation. David regarded his angulated friend. Kurt was hiding something. The feeling was almost physical, like a book out of place or a picture hung slightly askew.

"David?"

"Yeah, Kurt."

"Thanks, pal."

"For what?" David answered, sounding stupid to himself. "I mean, what are friends for?"

"I'm serious." Kurt tipped his chair back onto the floor. "I don't know what I was thinking when I got you mixed up in all this. I guess I was a little desperate. It could get a little dicey from this point on. This isn't your fight and it's not fair to ask you to take it on."

"Are you saying I'm off the case?"

"No strings, no regrets." Kurt was on his feet. "You've earned your plane ticket. Now it's time to have us some fun."

"Now hold on a second. I appreciate your belated consideration, but the fact is, I'm already involved. Besides my professional curiosity has been aroused. Don't freeze me out now, not when it's just getting interesting."

"You goddamned lawyers all think you're Perry Mason, don't you?" Kurt leavened his comment with a laugh. "Just do me a favor. Promise me you won't do anything without telling me first. You find out where the M-1s are keeping her and that's it. My dad's people take over after that."

Kurt extended his hand. "Deal?"

David gave it a long, firm shake.

"Great," Kurt said, indicating the subject was closed. "Now let's forget all this serious stuff. I'm having drinks tonight with some folks I'd like you to meet."

"Ah, I don't think so," David said with a yawn. "Not tonight. Jet lag. You go ahead."

Kurt looked like a doctor who had just lost a patient. "Okay, pal," he said as he pulled on his jacket. "You're off the hook this time. But tomorrow you're getting the city-lights tour. Don't go getting soft on me just because Andrea stomped on your nuts."

"Don't worry," David answered. "My nuts are just fine."

"I sure hope so," Kurt called out before slamming the front door. "Because you're going to need them."

David had lied about being tired. He needed some time alone. He went out to the deck and gripped the railing, as if bracing himself against the rhythmic sloshing of the surf. The sea at night had always unnerved him. It was as if, deprived of light, water became a different element, one that threatened to take back what it gave by day. The glistening black tide seemed hungry for the land as it clawed the sand in slow hissing spasms of possession and release. Garbage, small objects, even people, could be swept up and swallowed by the current, only to reappear later in another place.

Back inside, he fought off the urge to call Andrea again. Instead, he found the booklet he had taken from the church that afternoon. Despite the archaic language, the story had captured his imagination. What would the boys at the office think? He could almost hear Bragin making some crack about born-again lawyers or a possible custody battle between the Virgin Mary and the Holy Ghost. Right now, he really didn't give a shit what they thought.

The little pamphlet was still folded back to the page where he had stopped reading. He leaned back on the couch and began right after the part where the Bishop had demanded a sign.

. . . Juan Diego went back to the Most Holy Virgin and gave her the Bishop's reply. As soon as the Lady heard it, she said, "That is all very well, my little son. You shall return here tomorrow for the sign he has requested. Then he will believe and no longer doubt or suspect you. And mark well my words: I shall repay you for all the worry, work, and trouble you have undertaken on my behalf. Run along now, for tomorrow I shall be waiting for you here . . ."

The next day, when Juan Diego was to take the sign which was to convince the Bishop, he did not keep the appointment. For upon arriving at home the night before, he found that his uncle Juan Bernardino had become ill and was in danger of dying. Don Bernardino had gone to see a doctor, who relieved the suffering. During the night, Juan Diego's uncle asked that he go well before daybreak to Tlatiloco to bring a priest to hear his confession and prepare him for death, knowing that his time was at hand and he would never get better.

So before dawn Juan Diego was already en route to Tlatiloco for a priest. As he approached the road that passes at the side of the little hill at Tepeyacac toward the west, which was also his usual route, he said to himself, "If I take the direct path, the Lady may see me, and I must not be detained by the sign she has prepared for the Bishop. First I must hasten for a priest to get this anguish over with, for my poor uncle is surely waiting anxiously." So Juan Diego took another path around the hill. He thought this would prevent his being seen by her, who always sees everything, everywhere. Nevertheless, he saw her coming down from the top of the hill, and saw that she was looking toward the place where he had seen her twice before. She approached him and said, "What is the matter, my little son, where goest thou?"

Juan Diego bowed before her in greeting and replied, "My Lady, it will grieve you to hear what I have to say. A poor servant of yours, my uncle, is very sick. He is down with the plague and about to die. I am hurrying to your house in Mexico to fetch one of Our Lord's beloved priests to confess and prepare him to meet Our Savior. But even so, I will return right away to deliver your message. My Lady, please excuse me and be patient with me in the meantime. I shall not deceive you. Tomorrow I shall come here in all haste."

After hearing Juan Diego's words, the Most Merciful Mother spoke: "Listen and understand well, my son, that you have no cause to be frightened. Let nothing worry or afflict you further, not even the sickness of your uncle, for he shall not die now. (And at this moment his uncle was restored to health, as Juan Diego was to discover later.) When Juan Diego heard this from the Lady of Heaven, he was much consoled and became contented. He implored her to send him off without delay to the Bishop with the token or sign to ensure his belief.

The Lady of Heaven bade him go to the top of the hill at the exact location of their previous encounters. She told him that he would find there many flowers, some of which he should gather and bring back to show her. This was a place

74

where flowers never grew, for as it was hard and stony, it usually produced nothing but thistles and thorny plants, nopal cactus and mesquite. Juan Diego went immediately up the hill, and when he reached the top he was greatly surprised at the number and variety of Castilian roses blooming out of season, that time of year being frosty and cold. They were very fragrant and, covered with the dew that had fallen during the night, looked like precious pearls. He set about picking and gathering them and placed them within the fold of his outer garment.

Juan Diego hurried down the hill with the roses and stood before the Lady of Heaven. She took them into her hands and then returned them, saying, "My little son, these various roses are the proof you shall take to the Bishop. You are my ambassador most worthy of confidence. I strictly order you not to unfold your outer garment or reveal its contents until you are in the Bishop's presence. You shall tell him everything very carefully so as to convince him to give his help toward building the temple I want here." After the Lady of Heaven had finished her instructions, Juan Diego set out on his journey along the causeway that leads to Mexico. Contented and feeling sure that this time all would go well, he held his precious burden close, to protect it and to prevent any of its contents from falling out, meanwhile delighting in the fragrance of the various and beautiful flowers.

When he arrived at the palace of the Bishop, the major-domo and others of the prelate's household stepped out and interrupted his progress. He implored them to inform the Bishop of his presence, but they all refused, pretending they did not hear him. After Juan Diego had been standing there a long time, head lowered, with nothing to do, they noticed that he seemed to be carrying something. They went over to where he was and tried to see so as to satisfy their curiosity. The more Juan Diego resisted, the more they insisted. Since he saw that he couldn't hide what he carried from them, and fearing that they might tease, push, or strike him, he opened the folds of his garment a tiny bit. When they saw that he was carrying the roses of Castile, all of them different and blooming out of season, they were greatly amazed. They tried to take some of them away from Juan Diego. Three times they attempted, and three times they failed, for when their fingers closed upon the roses, they no longer saw real flowers but flowers which seemed to be painted, embroidered, or sewn onto the inner surface of the cloth.

Thereupon they went to tell the Bishop what they had seen and that there was a poor Indian who had been waiting a long time, the same one who had come before. Hearing this, the Bishop suddenly realized that this was the proof needed for him to believe and carry out Our Lady's wish. He immediately ordered the messenger shown in, and upon entering, Juan Diego knelt before the Bishop as he had the other times, repeating all that he had seen and marveled at, and the message. He said, "Seigneur Bishop, I did as you ordered, telling my mistress, the Lady of Heaven, Saint Mary, the precious Mother of God, that you wanted a sign to believe me when I told you that you are to build a temple at the place where she wished it. She yielded to your hesitation, receiving kindly your request for proof, and immediately sent me up the hill, where I had seen her before, to gather Castilian roses. She told me to bring them to you, and this I do. Behold them here. Receive them." And Juan Diego opened his white mantle, which up to then he had held close to his bosom. As soon as all the different roses of Castile fell and scattered on the floor, there suddenly appeared drawn upon the cloth the beautiful image of the Ever Virgin Saint Mary, Mother of God, just as she may be seen to this day in her temple at Tepeyacac, under the name of Guadalupe. Upon seeing it, the Bishop and all those present fell to their knees, regarding it with admiration for a long while, greatly moved by what they saw . . .

David put down the pamphlet and listened for a while to the melancholy sloshing of the sea. Of course, Juan Diego's unshakable faith seemed ludicrous in a secular age of high-tech superconductors, gene splicing, and MIRV nuclear warheads. But David knew that visions of the Virgin continued to occur in countries of the Third World. Logic told him that nothing was impossible, no matter how farfetched. Did Josefina see the story of Juan Diego as inspirational fiction, or as irrefutably true as the material world that he took for granted?

He decided to watch some TV before turning in. David clicked on the set and restlessly flicked the channels, settling on a *Star Trek* episode in which the crew of the *Enterprise* battle an alien being that can disguise itself by taking on the form of anything around it. As he gradually lost consciousness, David's thoughts drifted back to Josefina Juárez—a comely girl like that, living alone and in fear in a foreign country. What did she think about as she passed the hours in that tiny room? What did she ask for when she prayed to God? What had His answer been? Like the waves heaving under the moonless night, there was something about her plight that went deeper than its dark surface, deeper than friendship or the fate of a missing housekeeper, deeper than the fitful sleep that overtook him.

4

David dreams. An inviting scene, postcard bright, comes into focus: He is standing on a pristine white beach. The balmy air is like silk against his cheeks and legs. A dolphin dances in the water, riddling the limpid waves. He watches it dive in and out of the spray in an oscillating pattern of pure motion. As he looks on, the dolphin becomes a woman with long black hair. She comes toward him and smiles. They are walking together, letting the pearly wash caress their toes. David is experiencing the happiest moment of his life. He knows he could easily spend the rest of eternity gazing at this ocean, walking with this woman. The girl begins to sing, and her song is the music of seagulls flying, smooth black stones and the curl of waves splashed to diamonds in the wind.

David notices a figure standing farther down the beach. As they draw near, he can see it is a man dressed as a clown, juggling coconuts. The girl points at the clown and begins to laugh. The clown has black eyes and a painted smile that frowns when he puckers his lips. Glad to have an audience, the clown begins to do some tricks. He pulls a rainbow out of his hat, then a writhing fish. He waves his gloved hand and the girl disappears. After a while, David realizes she's not coming back and decides to look for her. But when he turns to leave, the clown follows, mimicking his movements. No matter what David does, the clown echoes him. Exasperated, David tries to push the clown away, but the clown only pushes back. He runs and the clown waddles in pursuit. He stops and the clown freezes in his tracks. When David tells the clown to leave him alone, the clown laughs, exposing a row of rotted yellow teeth. David punches the clown, but the clown responds by hooting and sticking out his tongue. This only makes David want to hit him again. With each blow, some of the clown's whiteface rubs off, exposing patches of dark skin. A crowd has gathered to watch the beating, gawking with open mouths. Soon they are cheering David on. The harder he hits the clown, the more paint comes off. The clown is bleeding by the time David recognizes his own face.

The *L.A. Times* building was downtown on a nondescript plaza next to City Hall. David craned his neck up at the stubby white tower and was reminded of the reruns of *Dragnet* that came on after the local news. Compared to the postmodern funk of Venice and Melrose Avenue, this part of the city seemed archaic and steadfastly quaint, like a sleepy Midwestern metropolis that had suddenly been transported into the twenty-first century.

As David parked his car and dredged his pockets for change to feed the parking meter, he was unaware of how close he was to Josefina's first bittersweet taste of Los Angeles. By some quirk of luck or clairvoyance, he might have decided to take a short detour into the dilapidated center of the city, where the lower classes hunted for bargains before rushing back to the sweatshops and factories that lined the area around Ninth Street and Olympic. Standing there, he might have spotted another girl who looked just like Josefina and wondered where she was going with the small cardboard box she had resourcefully fashioned into a suitcase, with a piece of rope for a handle, holding it close to her breast because it contained her only possessions in the whole world. All except for the crumpled wad of American dollars that she had wedged inside her bra, blushing when she did it because, even though it was the safest place she could think of, doing so reminded her of the whores that plied their sex for a few pesos to drunk gringos in Tijuana. Watching her hesitate on the curb outside the Million Dollar Theater, David might have had trouble understanding why she had paid a small fortune to be treated like chattel and dumped in the desert to fend for herself; why she had mutely boarded the Greyhound bus for the three-hour ride into the center of town, where she would scramble for a place on the bottom rung of a society that dismissed her as one more potential welfare recipient; why she had stayed.

"You may never find your way out again without a compass, but Max Rogers's desk is somewhere in that direction," the tanned receptionist said with a knowing smile, gesturing toward the far end of a maze of prefab partitions. "If you're not back in an hour we'll send out a search party."

"I'd appreciate it."

The *Times* newsroom seemed more like a vast accounting firm than David's image of a major metropolitan daily. There was no sign of sweating reporters in a deadline frenzy, no screaming, cigar-chomping editors, only carpeted cubicles and the discreet tapping of computerized word processors.

"David, over here." Rogers was waving from behind a wall of color-coordinated file cabinets. "You have to be an investigative reporter just to find the right desk in this place."

"I noticed."

They had met on the debating team during their junior year of high school. Max's regular partner was sick that week and David had just transferred over in search of an easy elective. Bespectacled and high-strung, Rogers was a self-proclaimed "Fabianist revisionary," which was variously interpreted by his peers as referring to a religious cult or the fifties teen heartthrob. An A student who hated school and a Jew who loved ham and cheese on whole wheat, Rogers had a reputation for institutional irreverence which was well-established by the time David crossed his path. Rumor pegged him as the mastermind behind a successful effort to get a ventriloquist's dummy on the ballot for student-body president. John B. Goode had come in second on a platform calling for coed football and the end of puppet regimes in Southeast Asia. That year's debate topic concerned whether or not the federal government should be required to provide funds for environmental protection. Max had persuaded David to incorporate a plank in their affirmative case that called for raising money by the legalization and taxation of marijuana. Their unorthodox form of financing didn't win them any trophies, but it did make them minor celebrities at the statewide forensic finals. After majoring in English at Berkeley and writing two unpublished novels, Max opted for a job at what he called "the word factory."

"Stop the presses," David said, pretending to unplug Rogers's computer terminal. "I just heard on the radio that God is dead."

"That's old news," Max retorted. "I wrote that obit years ago."

"You and Nietzsche. On deadline?"

"Always." Max leaned back in his swivel chair. "But that doesn't necessarily mean I'm busy."

They reminisced for a while about old times. Then David took the plunge and told Max about Josefina and the M-1 boys.

Max responded by turning to his computer and typing away at the keyboard. "Let's ask Mr. Know-it-all," he said.

The screen blinked and Max peered at the luminous characters. "We don't have a whole lot on these guys," Max said, punching another button. "Wait a sec. This is interesting. A couple of years ago, there was an effort to unite all the

Chicano gangs in East L.A., a sort of sawed-off United Nations. Failed, naturally. But the gangleader behind it was a certain Huero Maldonado."

"The leader of the M-1 boys," David interjected.

"You know, David, I really think you've got Pulitzer potential."

"Max, what do you know about Randall's re-election?"

"Only what I read in the papers."

"This is off the record?"

"Deepest throat." Max traced an X over his heart.

"The girl—Josefina. She was his maid."

Max's eyebrows levitated over the frames of his glasses.

"Would you make a copy of that clip on Huero?" David asked. "You can't use any of this, but if something printable comes of it, I'll make sure you're the first one to get the scoop."

"What, no exclusive?"

"I thought that only happened in the movies?"

"You're right," Max said. "Nothing's exclusive anymore —we're all logged on to the same data bank."

"Just do me one more favor and let me know if anything else turns up on Randall, the M-1s, or the girl."

"You got it." Max scribbled a name and number on a piece of paper. "Here. This guy might be able to save you time getting in touch with the M-1s. He's been a pretty good source on a couple of stories. Gang violence. Immigrant labor. He knows the barrio like the back of his Chevy."

David read the name. "Danny Ortiz. Thanks, Max. You can reach me at this number."

"David?"

"Yeah, Max?"

He was looking at David askance, twirling the eraser end of a pencil in his ear. "This isn't your usual beat. What's your stake in this?"

"No comment."

"Have it your way. I just want you to realize . . ." Max

picked his words carefully. "I want to warn you not to get your hopes up too high. If this girl is an illegal, she could be virtually anywhere. These people live in constant fear of being arrested and shipped back to Mexico. One way of avoiding immigration is by constantly moving along the fringes. That makes them vulnerable to all kinds of predators. I'm talking rape, robbery, drugs. If she's as pretty as she looks in that photo, she could even be working as a prostitute."

"I'm aware of that possibility, but thanks for the warning."

David waited, knowing that Rogers wasn't finished.

"What else?"

Rogers shrugged.

"If she doesn't have a green card, there's no way of tracing her whereabouts. No social security number, no registered address. At this point, she's part of the underground, totally invisible as far as normal society is concerned. Officially, it's as if she never existed."

David's grandmother had a tree, an avocado, that he loved to climb as a boy. Cradled in its slender branches, he would pretend that he was the master of a huge forest, filled with treasure and magic spirits that lurked in the leaves. His grandmother also grew figs and Santa Rosa plums, tart green apples and pale-yellow lemons that she squeezed for her matchless limonada. It seemed to him that anything anyone could want was right there in her garden.

One day she told him that the avocado was smothering the young pear tree under its branches and that it had to be cut down. David begged her to spare it and sacrifice the pear tree instead.

"But I have many avocados that give me more fruit than this one, and only one pear," she explained.

"I don't care," he insisted. "This one is special."

"Está bien," she relented with a chuckle. "You have chosen this tree to live, so now you must take good care of it. As it grows big and strong, so will you, mijito."

David looked at it now, the one his grandmother had dubbed "David's tree," and felt a pang of affection. He laid his hand on the thick trunk and looked up, searching for a sign of the shiny green skins of ripening fruit, the buttery yellow meat enclosing the heavy seed of the next generation.

"Quién es?" he heard his grandmother calling. "Who's there?"

"It's me, Grandma. David."

He turned to see her stooped figure, a shovel clutched in her bony fingers. When David hugged her, he almost lifted her off her feet, and the lightness of her body froze his heart.

"Qué chulo, mi hijito," she wheezed in his ear. "How strong and handsome he is."

David's grandfather was waiting in the doorway when they reached the house. As David came closer, the old man let out a gasp of recognition.

"Hi, Tata. Cómo estás?"

They entered the cramped living room and David was embraced by the odors of chorizo, pan dulce, and cheap perfume. It was the smell of his childhood, of long summer days and salmon sunsets that lingered in the gathering dusk. On the warmest nights of July and August the adults would move into the garden to play cards by candlelight, while David and his cousins chased each other across the humid lawns, intoxicated by the darkness.

"How are you feeling, Grandma?"

She shrugged and sucked her cheeks in disgust. "Doctors. All they want is money." She tucked a strand of hair behind her ear. "Estoy cansada, mijito. Your grandma is tired."

Senator Randall's face appeared on the television screen. ". . . The future and livelihood of this state and indeed this nation," he was saying, "lies in the cultural diversity of its people . . ."

"And you, Tata. How are you doing?"

His grandfather opened his toothless mouth to speak, but could only manage a wet clicking sound. The effort made tendons in his neck stand out. "I can't . . ." he managed to hiss.

His grandmother looked at her husband and shook her head. "Ya no puede," she said sarcastically. "He can't do it. He sleeps and eats, that's it."

If she noticed David flush, she didn't let on. Instead, she said, "He's a good man—for a gringo."

It took David a second to realize that her last words were referring to the Senator. She kept staring at the screen, but the wrinkles in her face deepened with humor.

"Grandma, you crack me up."

"Mijito," she whispered in conspiracy. "Venga." She patted the sofa next to her.

"Dime. Tienes muchas novias? You have lots of girlfriends in Nueva York?"

"Sure."

"How many, mijito?"

"Ten."

Her eyes widened in amazement.

"Diez?"

"Yeah, diez," he repeated.

She let out a loud cackle and gripped his knee.

"Qué bueno," she said after she had controlled her laughter. "Ándale. Vaya con todas. You get married, mijito?"

"Never."

"Good," she announced. "Play around."

It was David's turn to laugh.

"Come here, mijito." She took his hand and led him out to the garden. "Aguacates muy altos," she said, pointing at the tree. "Very high. I can't reach. I'm too old. Help me, mijito."

She handed him an old broomstick with a loop of wire attached to one end.

"Where, Grandma? I don't see anything."

"Mira," she instructed. "Muy grandes."

David peered into the topmost branches, convinced that they held nothing. Then he saw them. A whole cluster hidden behind the flat, rubbery leaves. A little to the right, a second bunch twisted slowly in the breeze.

"Jesus," he said. "I need a fire ladder to get up there."

"Aquí, mijito." She motioned to the side of the house, where a ladder hung horizontally from metal pegs. He lifted it off the hooks and carried it over, careful not to bash into anything as he wheeled it around behind him. Leaning it against the old avocado, David gripped the ladder with one hand, balanced the pole in the other, and started to climb.

There was a time not so long before when doing this would have been no more daunting than riding a bicycle. Now he was chagrined to find himself as shaky as a trapeze artist who has lost his nerve, wishing he worked with a net. When he was about level with the TV antenna, David gingerly lifted his foot off the topmost rung, shifted his weight to a medium-sized branch, and wrapped his free arm around the trunk. Lifting the pole the final few feet, David nudged two of the green pendulums through the hoop and yanked downward. He heard a dry ripping sound, followed by a double thud from somewhere below.

"Bueno, mijito! Ahora los otros. Now the rest."

His grandmother's voice sounded faint and strangely earthbound. David took another careful step and straightened up through an opening in the leafy canopy. From here he could see the irregular squares of the neighbors' back yards, a snaking section of the freeway, and, off in the distance, the smog-shrouded base of the San Bernardino Mountains. He felt calm and slightly giddy as he extended the pole toward the second bunch. Again, he lassoed two of the lobes and yanked. But this time the stems were tougher and yanked back, pulling the pole out of his hand and throwing him off balance. David teetered like a spastic Tarzan before managing to grasp another branch and hold on. He took a deep breath and looked down. His grandmother was standing directly under the tree with her arms stretched out, waiting to catch him.

The white cross floated against a range of low brown hills fading into the sun-bleached horizon. The phrase EN MEMORIA DE NUESTROS HERMANOS was painted above it, and below, inches from the sidewalk, THOUGH I WALK IN A BARRIO OF DARKNESS, I FEAR NO EVIL FOR GOD IS WITH ME. David had to look hard to make sense of the second sentence because an unconscious man in a torn undershirt lay sprawled across the words IS WITH ME, a brown paper bag welded to his hand. David watched as an old man with white whiskers pushed a Snow-Kone cart past the tragically embellished mural, calling "Raspadas, paletas!" He shuffled past the snoring drunk without slowing his gait or averting his eyes, which seemed fixed on a point ahead of him, thousands of miles away from the Maravilla projects.

David got out of the car and locked it, unable to shake the feeling that he was being watched. As he crossed the street, the scrape of his loafers on the pavement seemed deafening.

Like most public-works projects, the assortment of one- and two-story apartment blocks rejected any relationship with the surrounding neighborhood. Instead of the festive greens, yellows, and pinks that adorned even the shabbiest houses across the street, Maravilla was cloaked in an institutional beige. Instead of thriving jungles of succulent cacti and herbs, it was landscaped with crew-cut shrubs and barren lots of brown grass garnished with trash and empty beer bottles. Prideful poverty replaced by garbage-bin conformity, individual misery traded for the collective wasteland. Even so, David allowed, the people who lived here probably considered themselves lucky.

The afternoon sun bore down as he searched for the right unit, and soon his collar and armpits were soaked. As he looked in vain for someone to ask for directions, he was struck by the ghost-town ambience of the place, half expecting to see a mangy ball of tumbleweed roll by. Instead, he saw a little girl clad only in her underwear, her tongue stained crimson by a melting cherry Popsicle.

"Do you know where Johnny Benítez lives?"

She took her finger out of her mouth and pointed. First in one direction, then the other.

"Do you speak English?" he asked.

The girl shook her head.

"Hablas español?"

"Yes."

He was about to concede defeat when his ears picked up the strident whine of an electric guitar. He followed the music to its source, knowing that Johnny would be there, his head thrown back in Carlos Santana rapture as he coaxed the notes out of the Fender Stratocaster. They had had a date to jam the night of the accident, but Mondo had gone ahead and called a meeting of the Falcons.

"Johnny," David shouted through the open window, "I hear the Stones are looking for a new guitarist."

"That you, Davie? Son of a bitch!"

Johnny held the door open, then backed his wheelchair up so David could come in. They embraced, and for a moment David thought Johnny was going to pull himself to his feet and slap him on the back, the way he used to when they were kids.

"It's good to see you, Johnny-boy," David lied. "Nice little place you've got here."

"It's a fucking shithole," Johnny said as he pulled out a pack of Bambu papers and started to roll a joint. "But my sister lets me stay here for free."

"I guess that counts for something."

"Only when you're broke," Johnny observed dryly. "I'm

gonna get my own place again as soon as I get my next check. I've been looking out by City of Commerce." He lit the joint. "Man, you look great. It's been too fucking long."

"Yeah, too long," David said, making his eyes unfocus until the wheelchair became a formless blotch of gray. "Too long."

It begins in a way on Christmas Day. The bike is waiting for him in the living room, just as David knows it will be. The polished chrome handlebars gleam under the tree, scattering the early-morning light over the floor and walls. David never fails to get the biggest and most expensive toys on the block, and it doesn't take him long to learn that letting other kids play with his toys is an easy way of making and keeping friends. That morning David can't wait to take the bike out for a test drive. Careful not to alert his sleeping parents, he stealthily rolls it into the front yard, and before long it has attracted a small crowd of less-fortunate admirers. No one on the block has even heard of a five-speed Sting-Ray, let alone ridden one.

"David, let me ride it."

"No, David. Let me."

A small dark boy named Mondo pushes his way to the front of the group. He is first to notice the name stenciled on the green metal-flake body.

"Falcon. That sounds really bad, man."

By the end of the day, it has become the definitive word in the English language. They can taste its power as they roll it over their tongues, repeating it to each other like a mantra.

Falcon.

Somebody comes up with the idea that anyone who has ridden the bike is automatically inducted into a special club and that the name of the club is the Falcons. As a reward, Mondo is the first to ride. Then Johnny. By mutual agreement, the three boys become the leaders of the group. Johnny is soft-spoken, athletic, and well liked. Taller than David or Mondo, he has a tendency to stoop, even though his father, an electrician named Frank, is constantly ordering him to "walk like a man." Mondo is a lot harder to figure out. Short and muscular, with heavy Indian features, his willingness to do crazy stunts on his bike or accept any dare has earned him a reputation for fearlessness. No one knows much about him except that he lives with his aunt in a small apartment at the end of the street. The fate of Mondo's parents is a constant subject of speculation among the Falcons. Octavio says that his dad told him Mondo's father was put in jail for drugs. Somebody else says that they heard Mondo is an orphan who had been abandoned on his aunt's doorstep in a cardboard box. Even Johnny, who has known Mondo since kindergarten, doesn't know for sure. David tried to find out once, but Mondo deflected the question. "I don't have one," he replied quietly. "You guys, the Falcons, are my family." After that no one has the guts to ask again, and the mystery of his origins only adds to his dangerous aura.

The Falcons hold regular meetings behind David's garage, mostly for the purpose of smoking cigarettes and planning doorbell-ringing raids on neighboring blocks. David usually instigates the plans, with Johnny going along and Mondo making sure it actually happens. At Mondo's insistence, their nocturnal sorties become more ambitious. Meanwhile, at school, several Falcons are suspended for fighting during recess, and when a fire in the cafeteria breaks out the following night, word gets around that the gang was behind it. The next day, David detects an added measure of respect in the eyes of his classmates. It doesn't hurt that, despite his association with the Falcons, he is maintaining an A-minus average and took first place in the science competition. Through Johnny, other students begin to approach David, offering favors and loyalty in return for special protection from the Falcons. David and Johnny become the de facto leaders of the gang, reaping maximum reward with minimum risk. They hardly notice that Mondo is withdrawing from them and moving closer to a group of boys who never bother to come to school. David feels protected by the Falcons, accepted by his teachers. In class, he is careful to pronounce his name with an Anglo accent, and whenever people ask, he pretends not to understand Spanish. With certain people, he even begins to deny he is a Falcon.

The BB gun is no big deal at first, just something to point at bottles and an occasional sparrow stupid enough to fly over David's garage. To get in on the fun, a few of the other guys buy BB guns, too. That's when Mondo starts organizing "commando raids" on the neighborhood streetlights. David and Johnny are opposed at first, but their old pastimes pale beside the thrill of acting out *The Dirty Dozen* in their own front yards. Each bull's-eye is rewarded by a shower of glass exploding away from a small electric sputter. On nights when the Falcons are "on patrol" most of the other kids on the block tend to stay indoors, afraid of becoming handy targets. In time, the sidewalk guerrillas grow adept at dispersing at the first sign of trouble or the cops, only to regroup later at some prearranged spot. It's around this time that Johnny's dad buys him a secondhand Volkswagen hatchback. The afternoon that David and Mondo come over for their first ride together, Johnny has already stenciled FALCONS in green paint above the mudguards. Access to a car opens up a whole new world to the boys, who are now able to roam throughout the city. Before long, the other two get their own wheels. David opts for a stripped-down Ford van, Mondo for a vintage '57 Chevy with racing slicks and custom hydraulic lifts for optimum cruising on Whittier Boulevard.

As the Falcons discover drugs and girls, David can feel himself losing ground to Mondo's aggressive personality. Mondo becomes the gang's resident dealer, using the sale of pills and pot to win friends and supply himself with extra spending money. When David asks Mondo to cool it, he tells him to fuck off. "Some of us don't have rich parents to buy us anything we want," he sneers, and David feels his mouth go dry. Once equals who shared power, David and Mondo begin to regard each other with growing contempt. Behind his back, David starts to bad-mouth his former best friend as a loser, a small-time cholo without ambition or future. Mondo retaliates by calling David a "spoiled coconut" who has turned his back on his friends for a chance to kiss the asses of the pinche gabachos. Johnny, who always thinks of himself last, is split by opposing loyalties. It reaches the point where David and Mondo speak to each other only through their mutual friend, whose efforts to defuse the clash of egos are the only thing that keeps the Falcons from degenerating into warring factions.

Near the end of his junior year, David gets a call for a special meeting in a deserted warehouse over by the railroad tracks. The spot is on Mondo's turf, but David has no choice—to back out now is to abdicate his status as a Falcon. When David goes outside after dinner that night, Johnny is already there with a couple of the guys, quietly smoking a cigarette in the patio. Normally they would talk about girls and guitars on the way, but this time they set out without a word, Johnny leading the way through the underbelly of the city, a no-man's-land of deserted buildings and chain-link fences. They come to a large structure marked by an intricate latticework of broken windows. Mondo is perched on the crumbling steps with some members of his personal gang, their inky silhouettes blending into the darkness. Many of the faces are unfamiliar to David. They even dress differently; their hair is greased back into ducktails and they wear loose-fitting Pendletons over white T-shirts. One of them has a large switchblade tucked into his belt.

"I'm *so* glad you could make it tonight, hermanos," Mondo says when they reach the steps. "I guess you finished all your homework, eh?"

"We're studying primitive animals this week," David answers. "I figured this might count as extra credit."

"Listen to that, manos. Isn't he bright and sarcastic? I'll bet her makes a real good lawyer someday and makes us all very proud."

There are a few snickers from the Pendleton group.

"So he came here to learn something," Mondo continues. "I guess we're gonna have to teach him a lesson."

Kicking aside a door-sized sheet of metal, Mondo beckons for the others to follow. When some of the Falcons hesitate, Mondo mocks them, shouting, "What's the matter? Are you guys Falcons or chickens?"

David and Johnny are the last ones to climb in. The building is vacant except for a few drums of paint and scattered piles of lumber. The only light is a dim yellow glow filtering in through the skylights.

"So what's your big surprise?" David demands.

"Something really special."

"Oh yeah, how special?"

"Saturday-night special."

Mondo is holding the gun flat on the palm of his hand. "You want to try it out for a test ride, mano?"

"So this is your new toy," David says, painfully aware of the smallness of his voice.

Mondo begins to laugh, and his laugh says, *I've won, you're not one of us anymore.*

"That's real smart," David shouts. "All that's going to do is get you guys thrown into jail." But his words are quickly swallowed by the shadows.

"We'll see about that, won't we, mano?"

"Yeah, we'll see," David answers, shamed into retreat. "I don't need this bullshit. I'm getting out of here before the man shows up. Anybody coming with me?"

The ensuing silence roars in his ears.

"I am."

Johnny.

"Good," Mondo says. "Let the two maricóns go." But Johnny's defection has made his victory incomplete.

"Fuck you, Mondo," David says.

One of the newcomers moves forward, but Mondo stops him. "It's okay." he says to their backs. "Let them go home to their mothers. But don't ever come back, because the Falcons don't fly with gallinas."

This time the whole group joins in the laughter.

"Good weed, eh?" Johnny took another drag off the joint, holding it in as long as possible before exhaling a cloud of blue smoke.

"Yeah, great," David told him.

A few weeks later, Mondo and a couple of Falcons try to rob a liquor store on Beverly Boulevard. Somebody tips off the police and two units are waiting in the alley when they show up to make the hit, forcing the would-be bandits into hasty retreat. Shots are fired and a passerby is wounded. Mondo and two cohorts are arrested a few blocks away at a taco stand, and the sages of the street have him serving a minimum of two years for armed robbery.

That summer Johnny trades his acoustic guitar for an electric and starts taking lessons from a guy he knows in a local band. David comes over sometimes with his new Gibson and they jam together, playing Beatles, Stones, Santana, and anything else they can pick up from records or the radio. Johnny has a clear, sweet voice, and on certain songs David sings along, filling in the harmonies. They talk about forming their own band and becoming famous rock stars. The big joke is that they'll call the band Saturday Night Special.

During David's senior year, he is careful to keep his distance from the Falcons. He thinks he spots Mondo's face once among the guys who hang out in front of Millie's, but he can't be sure. Besides, David is too busy practicing with Johnny and applying to colleges to worry about the old gang. Like the rusty Sting-Ray in his garage, the Falcons are part of his past. The guidance counselor at school thinks David's test scores and grades are good enough to get him into a first-rate college, maybe even Stanford. The thought of attending a university is as exciting as it is daunting.

"Go for it, man," Johnny urges him one night as they learn the chords to "Brown Sugar." "You're as smart as those gringo bastards. You're not a dumb shit like me. You can do it. You're going places."

"So are you," David protests.

Johnny shrugs and makes a funny face.

Two weeks before graduation, the news comes that Mondo is out of jail and back in the neighborhood. He sends word to David and Johnny that he'll be looking for them after the big dance on Thursday night. David is relieved at first; to avoid a confrontation, all they have to do is not show up. But Johnny won't hear of it. "I'm not giving in to that bastard," Johnny tells him on the phone. "He's trying to make us look chicken again. Don't worry, Davie. He won't try anything; he's not *that* stupid."

David misses school the next day and spends the afternoon in his room reading and listening to records. He pulls out his guitar and tries to play the songs that he and Johnny have worked out over the past few weeks. After a few minutes he unplugs the amplifier. He needs Johnny backing him up to sound really good.

"I'm going to the dance," David announces at dinner.

"Not tonight," his father commands. And, for once, Susanna does not contradict him.

"If there's trouble," she says, "I don't want my boy hurt by a bunch of pachucos desgraciados."

"But I've got to show up," David pleads. "Johnny'll be alone."

"Better him than you," his father says. "You're not leaving my sight, understand?"

He tries to call Johnny at his house, but there's no answer. David has a plan. At dinner, he pretends to throw a tantrum, flinging his fork across the table. Predictably, his father cuffs him and orders him to his room. It seems as if his parents will never leave the kitchen, but finally they do. When their voices move to their bedroom, he slips out the window and starts running. He runs until his lungs are burning and every breath is agony, but he doesn't dare slow down. He is only a block away now. Johnny will be inside dancing, laughing at his friend's concern. So what if he gets grounded for a year; David can deal with his parents afterward.

As soon as David rounds the last corner and starts down the block, he knows something is wrong. There are people standing around outside the gym and the dance-floor light show is spilling into the parking lot. As he comes closer, David understands that the flashing lights are coming from an ambulance. Fighting a wave of nausea, he pushes his way through the crowd just as the paramedics hoist Johnny up onto the stretcher.

"What happened?" David asks, trying not to cry.

"I can't feel my legs."

"What the hell happened?"

"Mondo thought we finked on him, Davie. He said we tipped off the cops." Johnny's features were clouded by pain and disbelief. "Why would he think that?"

"I don't know," David says, and helps them close the door.

"Are you sure you're getting stoned enough, man?" Johnny was staring at him through the miasma of pot smoke.

"Yeah, it's great stuff. Really good."

Johnny seemed reassured. "I hear you're a big-shot lawyer now. You still like it in New York?"

"It's no big deal." David waved away the joint. "How about you, Johnny-boy?"

"Me? I'm hell on wheels, man." He stubbed the roach in a ceramic sombrero ashtray. A miniature Mexican dozed against the ash-filled brim, his feet darkened by a glaze of nicotine and marijuana resin. "I get by. I've got my guitar and my stereo. My sister cooks for me. That's about it."

"I'm looking for a girl, Johnny. This is a picture of her."

Johnny scrutinized the snapshot. "Not bad. Did she split on you or something?"

"It's not like that. She might be in trouble with the law."

Johnny shrugged. "Everybody around here is in some kind of trouble."

A fly danced on the window screen and Johnny made a halfhearted attempt to swat it with a newspaper.

"Fucking moscas! I can't get them on the ceiling. I need a swatter with one of those telescope things on the handle, you know?"

David nodded, trying not to look at Johnny's wasted legs.

"I've never been back East. New York must be a total trip. Big buildings and all that."

"It's pretty different," David agreed. "You'll have to get your lazy ass out there sometime."

The fly gave up on the window and started buzzing through the room, forming concentric circles over their heads.

"Your playing sounds really good," David said. "You've gotten better since the last time I heard you."

Johnny's face brightened. "I've had plenty of time to practice. I still miss those jams we used to have. We'll have to do it when I come out to New York. Maybe we can get back into the groove again."

"Maybe we can. Listen, what do you know about the M-1 boys?"

Johnny was flipping though his record collection. "They practically own the neighborhood. Sometimes they help people, sometimes they waste them. They're sort of the law around here."

"What about their leader, a guy named Huero?"

"Have you heard the new Santana album?"

"No. Put it on."

Johnny wheeled over to the stereo and carefully placed the record on the turntable. He wiped the grooves with a Disc-washer before setting down the needle.

"He's an intense dude. From what I hear, he's a little crazy, like Mondo, only smarter. I think he went to college."

The speakers pumped Latin rock into the room.

"You still dig this music?"

"Yeah, I do."

Johnny held out the album jacket and David noticed a crooked line of pimples or small sores running down his arm. Johnny looked up and saw that David knew.

"Don't judge me, man," he said.

On the way back to the car, David saw another mural. This one was a life-sized rendering of the Virgin outlined in Day-Glo orange tongues of holy flame. The artist had added bouquets of roses and marigolds under her feet. Only when David was much closer did he realize that the flowers were real.

5

There were no murals on the houses along Benedict Canyon Drive, where David left his car keys with the parking attendant before mounting the scalloped marble steps and squeezing through the crowded doorway of a peach-colored mansion. Back at the apartment, David had showered and changed into black jeans and a fresh shirt after finding a note from Kurt with directions to the party. "P.S.," Kurt's message had ended. "Ignoring this is not an option."

David sauntered through the main house, which was generously stocked with the best brands of booze, food, and bodies. Though it was barely eight o'clock, the party had obviously been going on for hours. The action was centered in an enormous glass-walled room that looked out over the manicured grounds. Two oversized posters of John Wayne and Karl Marx hung from the ceiling like banners above a knot of gyrating dancers.

Finding a bar, he ordered tequila and grapefruit juice from a servant dressed like the Lone Ranger.

"I didn't know this was a costume party," David said as he accepted his drink.

"It's Tex-Marx," the bartender corrected.

"What's that?"

"Texan-Marxist. You know, Gulag guacamole, Red Square dancing . . ."

David laughed. "And I suppose you're Deputy Dogma."

"Me? I'm the Red Star Sheriff," he replied, brandishing a crimson badge.

David turned his attention to the dance floor, where people were undulating singly or in odd-numbered groups to "La Bamba," then "Back in the U.S.S.R." Off in the corner of the room, two guys wearing Mao caps were playing Ping-Pong. A great cheer rose from the revelers as a motorized skylight rumbled open overhead, revealing the shaggy tops of spotlit palm trees.

David moved into the room, eavesdropping on random bits of conversation.

". . . I'd have to be shopping on the black market to get it at that price . . ."

". . . Do you realize that if you sleep with her you'll be sleeping with every extraterrestrial in the universe? . . ."

". . . It's getting to the point where I can't wear black without breaking into a horrible rash . . ."

". . . Well, whatever it is that never got started is finally over . . ."

". . . Did he pass the blink test? . . ."

"What's the blink test?" David asked.

He turned to see a man and two women staring at him. They seemed amazed that anyone would acknowledge their remark.

"Well," the taller woman explained as their little circle closed around him. "You pick a person out of a crowd and make eye contact until one of you blinks."

"Did I blink?"

"No."

"What would have happened if I had?"

"You would have lost," the man cut in.

"Lost what?"

"Whoever it was you were looking for."

"How do you know I'm looking for someone?"

The shorter woman cocked her head at him. "Everybody's looking for someone."

"Especially if they can't find them," the first woman chimed in.

The conspirators smiled.

"Is that right?" David said, spotting Kurt at the other end of the room. "Then it really won't matter if I leave, will it?"

"You blinked," the man said.

Kurt was drinking Campari-and-soda. "Nice group, eh?" he observed with studied detachment.

"If you say so."

"Them? They don't matter."

"Who does, Kurt?"

"See that blonde?" Kurt sighted along the rim of his drink to a starlet in a backless dress.

"Hard to miss her."

"She's dying to meet you."

"Could be terminal."

"I seriously doubt it." Kurt draped his arm over David's shoulders. "But first, the grand tour."

Kurt showed him the rest of the house, including the private gym and the billiard room. Then they strode out to the terrace, past a spouting fountain and onto a path that traversed the rolling lawns. Several guests were skinny-dipping in the triangular pool. "Come on in, the Perrier's fine," someone yelled.

"I'm impressed," David said. "Whose place is this, anyway?"

"He's a film producer's son. No talent, but can't face the cold truth."

"It doesn't look like he'll ever have to."

"It's the magic formula: wealth plus insecurity equals free entertainment."

The path dead-ended on the ridge of a steep cliff. Beneath them lay a dark expanse of winding canyons bordered by a latticework of estates and glittering boulevards that stretched out toward the seaside communities of Venice and Playa del Ray. The lights of the city sparkled like a close-up of the

Milky Way, creating the topsy-turvy illusion of looking down at a starry sky.

"I'm going to see Huero tomorrow," David announced.

"To make sure she's there?"

"Yup."

"Just remember our agreement," Kurt said gravely. "This is my fight."

"I remember."

They gazed out over the hills again in a mutual pact of silence. Kurt spoke without turning his head, his handsome profile defined by the urban afterglow. "You know, my family used to own some of the land we're standing on."

"What happened?"

Kurt let out a bitter laugh. "There are some lawyers in this town who are still trying to figure that out. I guess in the end you can chalk it up to the usual garbage. Family politics. An offer my granddad couldn't refuse."

"I never knew about that," David said lamely.

Kurt dug the heel of his shoe into the bluff. "When I was a kid I used to come up here alone sometimes. There was nothing around back then, just dirt and scrub and wild grass. It would take me half an hour and a gallon of sweat to get up here on my bike, but it was always worth it. There were coyotes at night and you could hear them yapping at the moon like maniacs. Scared the crap out of me, but that was part of the thrill. I used to stand here on this exact spot and feel like I owned the whole city, the whole world. I had my whole life in front of me and I knew it. And I knew that I knew it."

Kurt gave a short, cynical chuckle. "And then—I don't know why—something would snap inside and I'd feel sad. Not because anything was wrong; just the opposite—because I knew it could never be so right again."

Kurt kicked a dirt clod over the precipice and they both traced its trajectory into the void.

"When the developers started tearing everything up, I used

to pull out the surveyor's markers—those sticks with little red flags on them—and put rocks in the bulldozer's gas tank. But they kept on building houses, fencing the place off, piece by piece. Now the coyotes are gone and the assholes are the ones running wild. Rich people have no natural enemies—except maybe the IRS."

"Then again," David suggested, "nobody can really own land. I mean, as long as you can stand here and appreciate it like this, it's still yours in a way."

"I guess," Kurt conceded. "But the feeling's not the same."

David tried to imagine what the view must have been like before the city filled the great basin like a concrete cancer, before the real-estate boom, before the settlers and the Spaniards and the monks claimed it for themselves or their Queen or their God. Back when the Indians celebrated the land and magic, not money, was the highest power. Who paid the taxes, David wanted to ask, when everything was free?

"You're thinking maybe I lost something I never had," Kurt said, reading his thoughts. "But if that's true, then who owns it now?"

Kurt let the question twist in the air for a few seconds before adding, "So much for Zen and the art of surreal estate."

The spell was broken; their conversation evaporated like a mirage on a desert road.

"Yeah," David agreed. "I need another drink."

The dancing had spread beyond the skylight room to the rest of the house, and David and Kurt had to shield their cocktails from thrashing limbs as they circumvented the furniture. David heard a glass shatter, then a peal of throaty laughter. The blonde was standing alone by the buffet, oblivious to the ruckus going on around her. Probably sampling the Trotsky tortilla chips, David thought to himself. Before he could decide whether or not to approach her, he felt Kurt's fist in the small of his back propelling him forward.

"I don't believe we've met."

She took a sip from her drink and gave him an appraising glance. "Is that your idea of a clever line or something?"

"Just the facts, ma'am."

"Well, based on your Joe Friday, I know you're not an actor."

"Is that a drawback or an advantage in this town?"

"I also know you don't live in Los Angeles."

"You seem to know an awful lot about me," David said. "Maybe you should know my name. I'm David."

"And I'm Goliath," she said before disappearing into another room.

David decided it was time to make a pit stop. He wandered through the empty part of the house until he spotted a group of people queued up outside a door. He had just joined the line when somebody tapped him on the shoulder. It was a man in a tuxedo and lavender bow tie. "Excuse me," he said politely. "But do you mind if Miss Bennett goes in ahead of you?"

Miss Bennett was an elderly woman in a pink silk gown with ruffled feathers around the collar. Rhinestone earrings sagged from her lobes like overweight luggage.

"Sure." David gritted his teeth. "Be my guest."

The bathroom door was flung open and the three conspirators emerged with sheepish grins. The sink, toilet, and shower stall had been festooned with billowing strips of toilet paper. "Who's next?" they asked cheerfully.

David found Kurt on the terrace, standing with a clique of laughing people.

"Marty, I'd like you to meet my partner in no-collar crime from the Big Apple," Kurt said to a balding young man dressed in baggy white pants and a deafeningly loud Hawaiian shirt. "David Loya, meet Martin Jaffe, one of the most decadent men in the business."

"Kurt, you would make a marvelous press agent," Jaffe retorted, lifting his champagne glass. "It must run in the family. Oops, just a joke," he added, covering his mouth as if he had said something naughty.

"New York, hell of a town," Jaffe exclaimed as he returned his attention to David. "I once heard it described as ten pounds of shit in a five-pound bag."

"But it's really good shit," someone added.

"Absolutely. I meant that in a good way." Jaffe made a wobbly circle with his glass. "David, we were just discussing the most intriguing subject. It seems that a few years ago some scientist in New Orleans discovered the exact part of the brain responsible for the sensation of pleasure. There's a funny story behind it about some confused rats, but we'll skip that part and spare the squeamish. What's important is that this guy started implanting electrodes into the brains of humans, making it possible to stimulate this so-called pleasure center with the push of a button. You know: on/off, on/off. Imagine the implications."

"I think Woody Allen already did," David said.

"Conceivably," Jaffe went on, "we could dispose of all this expensive garbage that makes us feel good for about twenty minutes—booze, drugs, sex . . ."

"Movies," somebody shouted.

". . . and just carry around this little box."

"But then what would people grow in the jungles of Bolivia?" Kurt asked.

"Hey," Jaffe shrugged, "so we've got a few bugs to iron out!"

A burst of sit-com laughter arrived on cue.

"What's so bleeding funny over here?"

David didn't even have to look; it was the blonde.

"Trudy-puss," Jaffe cooed, pulling her close for a brotherly kiss. "I think you're well acquainted with this pack of jackals. And this gentleman here is Randall's friend from New York, David Loya."

"We've met," she said before David could open his mouth. Her grasp was firm.

"Well," Jaffe made his voice oscillate, "no introductions *needed* in this little group."

Jaffe traded a look with Kurt, who steered the conversation back to New York.

As he answered an inane question about the best restaurant in Manhattan, David saw Jaffe whisper into Trudy's ear and slip something into her hand. It was deftly done, like a card trick.

"Sorry, but I'm about to steal Mr. Loya away for myself," Trudy said, wrapping her arm around his and leading him upstairs.

"I know I must have seemed rude before," she apologized as soon as they were alone. "It's just that there are a lot of jerks running around in this place, if you know what I mean."

"I think I do."

She halted at what looked like an empty bedroom. Locking the door behind them, she opened her purse and pulled out a tiny straw and a plastic pouch filled with orange powder.

"Want some," she offered.

"Cocaine makes me jumpy."

"Cocaine? Nobody does that anymore. This is much more, um, compassionate."

"Maybe next time."

She shrugged and took a dainty snort. "Loya. Is that Portuguese?"

"My grandparents are from Mexico."

"It's just that I had a Portuguese boyfriend once. You look a lot like him, but taller."

She was pretty enough to be a model, except for her nose, which had a slight hook. She joined him where he was sitting on the bed and he could see her pupils dilating.

"Tall, dark, and handsome. Just how I like them."

She leaned over and put her lips on his. Her tongue seemed possessed.

"You know," she said, catching her breath. "I've got the keys to a great house in Palm Springs that no one's using this week. We could leave first thing in the morning."

"What's the hurry?"

"No hurry," she said as she unbuttoned his shirt. "I just think we could have a lot of fun together."

David couldn't shake the feeling that they were acting out some prearranged scene. Their conversation rang in his ears like dialogue from a B-romance. This was the part where he was supposed to reach over and put out the light.

Camera.

Action.

Cut.

"Listen," he said as she began to unbuckle his belt, "did Jaffe tell you to stimulate my pleasure center?"

"Does it matter?"

"It might."

"You could have fooled me," she said, running her fingertips over the bulge in his jeans.

"That's not what I mean. It's just not a very good time for me to be getting involved with anyone."

"Who," Trudy asked as she leaned over to switch off the light, "said anything about getting involved?"

The girl is older than David, about seventeen, he guesses, and doesn't even speak English. But the stuffy little house makes him squirm in his chair until his mother is forced to banish him to the back yard.

"Go play with your cousin, Lupita."

"She's not my cousin."

"Yes, she is. She's your second cousin. Now leave us alone so we can talk in peace."

David isn't sure what a second cousin is, but he doesn't much like the sound of, or the look of, this place. The blazing sun has bleached the color out of everything, and the dirt under his feet is as hard as concrete. The excitement of crossing the border into another country has worn off, and

David wishes he were back in his own neighborhood, where the streets have real sidewalks and the dogs aren't too tired or hungry to wag their tails. Lupe is feeding the chickens in a wire enclosure tucked in a corner of the yard. Her brown braids brush along the ground as she stoops among the tweeting chicks. There is nothing else to do, so David comes closer to watch the comical way that the birds scramble around pecking at anything in sight. He is astonished that people who don't live on a farm would be raising chickens. When they want to eat one, he wonders, do they take it to the butcher or kill it themselves? He is itching to ask but doesn't dare speak. He is still shy around girls, especially if they're taller than he. David once saw a man break a chicken's neck at a family barbecue. The sight of the hen being twirled on the end of its own bloody neck was a more violent spectacle than any cops-and-robbers shoot-out.

There are some newborns in the coop, and the way they queue up behind their mother, as if connected by invisible string, strikes David as very funny. Noticing that the chicks have caught his fancy, Lupe picks one up and lets him hold it in his hand. She puts some seed in his other hand and holds them together until the chick gets the idea. Its beak tickles his palm as it eats. David starts to laugh, and for a moment he forgets that he hates Tijuana.

Lupe asks him in Spanish if he wants to walk down to the grocery store for a Coke, and David says sure. Lupe and her family live in a colonia, although David would never think of calling it that. There are deep ruts in the street where the rain has formed small rivulets before spilling into a sloping arroyo at the bottom of the hill. They cross over a bridge and David sees a group of boys about his own age cavorting in the rust-colored water. Off in the distance, a few women are washing clothes on the muddy banks that separate the houses from piles of burning garbage. During the drive to Lupe's house, he saw so many smoldering dumps that he thought the whole city might catch fire.

The store turns out to be a tin shack that sells cigarettes, sundries, and soda. Lupe pulls two heavy coins out of her pocket and explains that they must drink their Cokes there or else pay for the bottles. This seems exceedingly strange to David, but he keeps his mouth shut. As they slake their thirst through skinny white straws, an old man with a silver tooth mutters something to David that he doesn't understand. Despite his curiosity, he doesn't like the way the man is smiling at them, licking his chops. David moves closer to Lupe and motions for her to hurry and finish her drink.

The adults are standing outside when they get back. Normally, wandering off without permission would be grounds for a whipping, but today is different. David is informed that Lupe and her mother are coming to stay with them until they can find jobs and a place of their own. To David this is tantamount to opening up their home to strangers, but there's nothing he can do about it. His dad adds some cardboard boxes to the suitcases in the trunk of their car, and they all pile in, his mother and father up front, with Lupe wedged in the back seat between David and her mother. As they approach the border, men loaded down with plaster donkeys and blankets run up to the car. David is relieved when his mother waves them away, saying, "I can't believe the gringos are dumb enough to buy that junk." Their car passes right through at the Mexican checkpoint but is stopped on the U.S. side, where a customs officer politely inquires if they are carrying any fresh fruit, plants, or fireworks. David closes his eyes, trying to wish away the firecrackers in his pocket. If they're using sniffer dogs, he's done for.

"No, sir," his father says.

"Are you all U.S. citizens?" the officer asks next, peering into the back seat.

His father says something about "visitors" and tells Lupe and her mother in Spanish to show their papers. For an agonizing instant David is worried that the customs man will ask to see his papers, too. "I'm an American," he blurts out, humiliated by the prospect of being mistaken for a Mexican. The guard smiles at him and, after looking over the documents, waves them on with a "Have a nice day, folks." David is seized by simultaneous waves of relief and loathing for the woman and her daughter, as if their very presence in the car has somehow tainted his family. He starts to hum "America the Beautiful," softly at first, then loud enough for everyone in the car to hear.

The sun goes down around the time they pass San Diego, and Lupe's mother lays a blanket down across their laps to keep their legs from getting cold. It is a long, monotonous drive and David spends the time thinking about his science project and hoping that he won't be forced to share his room. After a while, the grownups exhaust the possibilities of small talk and the only sound in the car is the steady hum of the engine and Lupe's mother's snoring. David is on the verge of sleep himself when he feels a hand touching his leg under the blanket. He cannot believe what is happening. The furthest he has gone with a girl is the time Mary Lou Bonner stuck her tongue in his mouth at her fifteenth birthday party. Johnny had warned him it might happen and he had taken the precaution of clenching his teeth. This, however, is an altogether different situation and he will have to improvise as best he can. Lupe's hand slowly moves up to his fly, and all he can do is swallow, paralyzed with sexual tension, afraid to open his eyes and acknowledge his unshackled erection, afraid that she will continue to urge him toward the threshold with firm, knowing strokes, afraid that she will stop.

The next day David pretends to be too sick for school, opting for a different sort of education. As soon as the adults have left for work, Lupe comes to his room, still dressed in her nightgown, and asks how he's feeling. I'm dying, he tells her. You're lying, she says, and begins to tickle him. He pins her to the blankets and holds her there as laughing becomes kissing becomes panting. Lupe pulls down his underwear and lifts her nightgown; she has lost the battle but won the war. As the Jesus on the crucifix over the bed looks on, Lupe spreads her legs and ends David's childhood. Anchored to her heaving body, David becomes an explorer charting the fleshy contours of a vast new world. She leads him between peaks of pleasure, over plateaus of abandon and withdrawal, until every motion is swallowed by a larger rhythm and David wonders who has entered whom.

Then David learns another lesson he will never forget.

"Do you love me?" she asks on his third day of lovesickness.

"Yes," David replies, certain for once of how to respond.

"Then we should get married."

David doesn't answer, but his mind is reeling from the consequences of what she has said, of what they have been doing. Shacks and starving dogs flash through his mind like scenes from a nightmare. Though he hardly knows it at the time, the idea of burying his mother's diamond ring in the back yard so that Lupe and her mother will be blamed for its disappearance is already germinating. That night he prays to God for forgiveness and help. But David knows that God isn't listening, and that even if He were, He would only feel the same disgust that David feels for himself. Besides, God will not help him get Lupe and her mother out of the house. So David stops praying and kneels instead at the altar of reason. And if it is a lower faith, at least it is custom-made for mortals, born as it is from the minds of impure men. Most important of all, to worship in this church David needs neither sacraments nor the Bible nor divine forgiveness. All he has to do is think.

David left the party without saying goodbye to Kurt; his friend could certainly take care of himself, and if not, Trudy would be more than happy to help. David was more concerned about his own well-being. It was unlike him to turn down such an easy score. Worst of all, his sudden attack of scruples felt spurious; it had become one more false note, one more step in the dance away from himself. The whole episode had only served to lower his self-esteem another notch. Easy virtue, it turned out, was no more of a panacea than easy sex.

David found the parking attendant and insisted on getting his own car. To reach it, he had to hike up the road a few hundred feet toward the crest of the hill. As the din of the party receded, his mind cleared and he began to feel better, his nostrils awaking to the fresh scent of wet grass. He stood motionless for a while, aware of the dew soaking his cuffs, letting the grating saw of crickets fill his ears, until the early-morning peace was broken by the mournful cry of a young drunk howling at the moonless sky.

"I was afraid I was going to get your answering machine again." He could hear Andrea breathing on her end of the phone. "We've got a pretty good connection, considering." He was stalling for time, anything to keep her on the line.

"I don't think so," she said flatly.

"Think what?"

"That we have a good connection—considering."

Touché. He had set himself up for that one.

"Where have you been the past few days?"

"None of your business. You didn't bother to tell me where *you* were going."

Her voice was constricted. David was almost relieved; anger was better than nothing at this juncture. "Andrea, all you had to do was call my phone machine to find out I was at Kurt's."

"Right. Your old Harvard chum. Has he set you up with any buxom volunteers yet?"

"No."

"Who *has* he set you up with?"

"Nobody you have to worry about."

"Did you call me to brag about your self-restraint with Hollywood bimbos?"

She was openly hostile now. He figured he had it coming. "No."

"So why did you call?"

"To say I'm sorry."

"Sorry about what?"

"Everything."

"Sorry isn't good enough, David. I need more than sorry."

"I miss making love to you." He knew it was true the instant he said it.

"So why did you run out on me? On us?"

"It's not that simple."

"How simple do you want to make it?"

"Andrea, I don't want to lose you."

In the wordless minute that followed, David could hear the hissing static of some cosmic disturbance, garbled bits of other conversations, muted buzzes, and stray beeps. He imagined their words moving at light-speed through the atmosphere, bouncing off a satellite in space, going nowhere.

"I don't want to lose you, either."

The doorman is staring at David as he fumbles through the pockets of his jeans and his corduroy coat and finally his overnight bag.

"I know I've got it here someplace," David says, as tiny beads of perspiration form on his chin.

"I'm sure it's there, sir."

He locates sunglasses, Chap Stick, a Swiss Army knife, a pack of lubricated condoms, and a small fortune in Greek drachmas—anything, it seems, except what he is looking for. David is about to give up, resigned to the humiliation of having to wait in the lobby, when the key slips out of the lining of his jacket and onto the plush carpeting.

"Could that be it, sir?"

It is only later, in the elevator, that David registers the condescension in the doorman's voice. Or is he just projecting his own sense of trespassing? He decides he's being paranoid. When Andrea first suggested they use her parents' apartment to "get away" for the weekend, he had balked, arguing that they would be uncomfortable or, more accurately, he wouldn't be comfortable vacationing amid the ostentatious display of Venetian glass vases, second-rate artwork, and first-rate antiques. Besides, what if her parents came home from Europe early and walked in on them while they were making love on the Danish rug in the living room? "They'd probably get off on it," Andrea had teased, calling him a "killjoy" until he finally relented. The plan was for Andrea to get here before him, but she had given him a key "just in case." Now he is paranoid and pissed off as he pads down the hallway, still feeling like some kind of cat burglar. Only after he gets the door open does he hear the elevator door whisper shut. They've been watching him, all right.

David locks the door behind him and surveys the spacious living room, trying to imagine a childhood amid such studied opulence. Of course, Andrea was in college by the time her family moved to the East Side. She had spent most of her formative years in Norwalk, one of the several "bedroom communities" in Connecticut within commuting distance of the city. It was a curious term, evoking an image of countless mattresses arranged in neat clusters around supermarkets and train stations. The same went for "summer houses" in the Hamptons. The idea of sharing vacation houses with total strangers had been a novel concept to him. It made a lot more sense after he had spent a sweltering summer in the city.

"Hello?" David calls out, fairly sure that he's alone. "Anyone the hell home?"

He puts down his bag and strolls through the rooms, gradually taking possession of the place, just as he has taken possession of Andrea. He is her lover, after all, and his presence in the apartment signals a tacit acceptance of that fact. Not that Andrea's parents have ever objected to his seeing their daughter. On the contrary, they have never been less than gracious and hospitable. They are also intelligent enough to know that any effort to control the life of their headstrong daughter would only make him that much more attractive to her. It isn't as if he's ready to pop the question or anything. Still, he can't help speculating over whether or not they would be pleased to have him as a son-in-law. Up to now, they have carefully avoided any discussion of his and Andrea's getting married. Of course, they could just be biding their time, secretly betting that, left alone, the relationship will eventually collapse under its own weight.

David reaches the master bedroom, pausing at the threshold. If he enters, his trespassing will no longer be an imagined act. What would they say if they knew he had invaded their private sanctuary? He pushes the door open wider and steps inside. Unlike the rest of the apartment, the master bedroom is ultramodern, a pristine environment of stark white surfaces. The effect is surprisingly severe, even chaste. Like everything else in the room, the dresser is spotless and bare, except for a single photograph of Andrea and her parents, the picture of domestic happiness. Or is it? The apparent perfection of the image makes him look closer. Andrea is facing the camera, smiling in that forthright manner that some people find intimidating. Mom and Dad, though, seem to be staring off in slightly different directions, their hands not quite touching. It's true that he can't imagine Andrea's parents making love, but who could blame him? He has always sensed a cool reserve lurking behind their impeccable manners. David moves to the king-size bed and has a perverse impulse to touch the cream-colored satin bedspread, running his fingers across the glossy folds of fabric.

"Wanna try it?"

Andrea is standing in the doorway, her face full of mischief.

"You scared the shit out of me."

"I love sneaking up on you."

"I was just casing the joint."

"Don't worry, I don't think you're a snoop."

"Hey, you were supposed to be here waiting for me," David says, suddenly remembering his anger. "I didn't particularly like getting the third degree from the doorman."

"I know. I'm sorry, darling." She puts her arms around him. "The hangers screwed everything up and I had to fix it before I left. Don't be cross. I'll make it up to you, I promise."

Her hands slide down his back and linger on his buttocks.

"How do I know I can trust you this time?" he says, becoming aroused.

"Because," she says, as she leads him to the bed, "my body never lies."

It's dark outside when David awakes. He knows he's been crying in his sleep, but he can't remember what it was that made him so sad. It doesn't make any sense; he has everything he ever wanted. He's young, he's got a gorgeous girlfriend and a promising future. A tear travels down the side of his face and soaks into his pillow. Then, just when he stops trying to make it happen, a fragment of the dream flickers through his mind: He is climbing a hill in a faraway place. There's a woman with him, but he has a vague impression it isn't Andrea. She speaks, but her words dissolve like a whiff of perfume in a crowded subway. David racks his brain, but there's nothing more. Where did the dream come from and why did it leave him staring at the wall with a dull ache in his chest? David lies motionless in the tangled sheets, listening for an answer as Andrea's rhythmic breathing is absorbed by the sounds of the sleepless city.

116

6

David stared at the illuminated menu and settled on a Taco Bell enchirito and a Coke. The girl behind the sliding window took his order by pushing some buttons in an enervated motion.

"You want hot sauce with that?"

"Doesn't it come with hot sauce?"

"Yeah, but you can't hardly taste it."

"Well, how hot is the hot sauce?"

"Not very."

"So what do you do if you want your food to taste really hot?"

"You order extra hot sauce."

"But you just said that it wasn't hot."

The girl tapped her foot on the ersatz-brick linoleum.

"Listen, mister, I just work here. You wanna talk to the manager?"

"Never mind. I'll take my chances."

David paid for the food and sat at one of the plastic picnic tables to wait for Danny Ortiz. The morning overcast had dissipated into an afternoon glare that made David understand why everyone in Los Angeles placed such a premium on owning a decent pair of sunglasses. He looked at his microwaved meal and felt a sudden wave of torpor. In Mexico, the hot sauce would be hot and this time of day would be siesta, a sensible custom of rest and consolidation before resuming the duties of the day. In fact, David would much rather have been taking a nap in a cool patio than wasting his time eating a prefab hybrid of Mexican food. His only consolation was the chance that his gastronomic suicide might lead him to Huero and, ultimately, Josefina.

"I give no guarantees," Ortiz had warned him on the phone that morning. "It's not like making an appointment with your local congressman." Then Ortiz had laughed and hung up.

David was still picking at his unsavory meal when a blue Impala pulled up alongside the curb. A short, ursine man sporting long sideburns and tortoiseshell Ray-Bans sat down at the table.

"Qué tal," Ortiz said, extending a hand.

David took it, finding himself in a brothers-style grip.

"Let's get this straight," Ortiz said with a broad grin. "You are representing Senator Randall, correct?"

"Let's just say I'm a friend, trying to help out."

"Titles are irrelevant, only actions count," Ortiz said. "Especially in these days of duplicity and corruption. Don't you agree?"

When David didn't answer, he just grinned, resting his hands on his paunch. "A man of few words. I like that. I am here to tell you that Huero will see you, but on his terms. You will come with me and leave your car here."

"Fine."

As David climbed into the Impala, he noticed a man half-way down the block simultaneously getting into a blue sedan.

"Hold it a minute," he told Ortiz, waiting until the car had pulled into traffic and kept going. David silently chided himself for being so jumpy. "All right," he said. "We can go."

As they drove north on Atlantic, they passed Our Lady of Guadalupe, and David turned, half expecting to see Sister

Ramona standing on the steps. They continued along a side street that ran parallel to the Long Beach Freeway overpass. David didn't need to ask where they were going: this was the route to M-1 territory. Ortiz took a left on Floral and slowed down. "This is Huero's turf," Ortiz announced, as if he were conducting the BarrioWorld ride at Disneyland. "He and his men control the whole area. Nobody comes or goes without him knowing about it."

"What about rival gangs?"

Ortiz raised the corner of his mustache. "There's White Fence and The Fobia, but they're not a problem. A few cholos have been wasted for being on the wrong side of the street at night, but that happens everywhere these days. It's the Viets and the Koreans that give us the most trouble. They are mean sons-of-slant-eyed-bitches. We have to teach them a lesson now and then. Show them who's top dog. Huero calls it 'antisocial Darwinism or survival of the baddest.' That's pretty good, eh?" Ortiz's belly shook as he made a hissing noise through his teeth. "Everybody in Maravilla knows who Huero is, and if they don't, they find out pretty fast. Forget about the man; after dark the M-1s rule. Huero is respected by the people. He is an educated man, a man of reason and substance."

David nodded diplomatically. "What about the illegals? Who protects them?"

"You mean the mojados. The wetbacks. Let me tell you something that none of the politicians understand. They can't be stopped, nobody can stop them. When a wet gets caught by the Migra, he just laughs and says to his wife, 'Goodbye, darling, I'll be back tomorrow.' And he comes back the next day—with two cousins and an uncle!" Ortiz slapped the steering wheel with his fist. "And it's not just us. The Orientals are coming, too. Monterey Park looks like we lost the Korean War, you know? All this politics about too many Mexicans coming over the border is pure bullshit. And I'll tell you why."

"Tell me."

"Because we never left!" Ortiz declared triumphantly. "This is *our* country, always has been. We're just letting the gringos stay here for a while. And, let me tell you, they owe us a lot of back rent!"

David noticed that Ortiz's smile had stretched into a leer. The expression heightened the Oriental cast of his features, and David was unnerved by the passing notion that Ortiz was speaking from behind a mask, his real face obscured by his expression.

The Impala halted in front of a low building with a hand-painted sign that read: LOS AMIGOS—*Engine and Body Work.* Several cars in various stages of disassembly obstructed the driveway like some sort of street-corner demolition derby. The corroded steel door was drawn back and two muscular men in white T-shirts watched as David and Ortiz got out of the car. Ortiz spoke to them in Spanish, too quickly for David to catch it. They were about to step inside when one of the men blocked their way, sending adrenaline pumping into David's system.

"Raise your arms," the man ordered. They complied and he frisked them expertly. Satisfied that they weren't carrying concealed weapons, the man stepped aside and nodded toward the rear of the garage. It was cooler inside and David was glad to be out of the heat for a while. In the middle of the room someone was working on the engine of a souped-up vintage Camaro. It was outfitted with racing slicks, and orange flame decals blazed from the fenders. The mechanic craned his head around the open hood and nodded in greeting.

"You must be Randall's errand boy," Huero said.

"His name is David Loya," Ortiz interjected.

"I'd shake your hand," Huero said pleasantly, "but I might get it all greasy." He stepped out from behind the car and held up his palms for David to see, at the same time flashing a row of straight white teeth. Huero's chiseled features were more Castilian than Indian, his shirtless torso lean and well defined. A coil of premature gray bisected his chestnut locks and David understood why he had been dubbed with the Spanish word for blondie. What surprised David the most, though, were the spectacles. Round and rimmed with gold wire, they gave him a sensitive, intellectual air. Ortiz had been right: this guy was no ordinary hooligan.

"A wedding present for my nephew," Huero said, indicating the car. "I'm partial to '66 Mustangs myself."

"I didn't come here to talk about cars, I came to talk about Josefina Juárez."

"He's come to talk about Josefina," Huero repeated thoughtfully as he adjusted the jaw of a wrench. "You know, that's funny, man. It's funny how people want to talk about Josefina now. Nobody gave a fuck about her a few weeks ago, did they? Now all of a sudden even politicians are interested. It must be her birthday or something." He looked at Ortiz as if to share a private joke. "What do you think, Homes? Maybe we should give her a party?"

"Simón." Ortiz let out a burst of mirthless laughter. Was he afraid of Huero, too?

"I haven't got time for jokes, especially bad ones," David said, trying to match Huero's cockiness. "You call the Senator and threaten to blackmail him. You say Josefina is with you but offer no proof. Why should anyone believe you?"

Huero tightened something in the engine. "That's a strong word, 'blackmail.' Almost as strong as 'rape.' You know that word, don't you?" Huero was toying with him, trying to get under his skin.

"What the hell are you talking about?"

"What the hell am I talking about?" For the first time David detected real menace behind the calm exterior. "Maybe you think Josefina got pregnant from playing with herself? Or maybe it was an act of God, like the Virgin Mary?"

"What do you mean?"

"I don't fucking believe this!" Huero hurled the wrench

into a stack of paint cans. "Randall sent you to deal with me and he didn't even tell you that the reason his favorite maid left so fast was because the son-of-a-bitch knocked her up? C'mon, man. You expect me to believe that? Do I look that stupid?"

David felt the enchirito trying to climb back up his throat. "I didn't know anything about that," he stammered.

Huero read the genuine shock on David's face, and his anger subsided. "It looks like your boss didn't tell you the whole story, my man."

"He's not my boss." David could barely get the words out.

"Then what is he, man? Your father? You look almost white enough to be his son. Maybe your mother used to be one of Randall's maids, too?"

"You don't scare me, Huero. I grew up around here, too. I've dealt with scum like you before."

"I'm impressed," Huero said with a smirk. "The Senator has sent us a homeboy, someone who speaks our own language." Huero was still smiling. "You know what a coconut is, right? Brown on the outside, white on the inside."

"Fuck you, Huero."

David felt sick with confusion and shame. Huero was pushing all the right buttons, trying to get him to crack.

"C'mon now, homeboy." Huero was laughing at him. "Is that any way to treat your hermano?"

"Let me talk to Josefina," David said, trying to get back to the point of his visit. "Even if what you're saying about the Senator is true, that doesn't give you the right to kidnap her."

"You know"—Huero was calm again—"you people are so full of shit it makes me want to puke." He wiped his hands on a rag. "Nobody kidnapped Josefina. Randall's boys were hassling her and she came to us for protection. She sure wasn't going to go to the police. They would have busted her ass back to Mexico like that." He snapped his fingers. "So she joined her people, where she belongs."

"What do you mean Randall's boys hassled her?" David felt as if the oxygen were being pumped out of the room.

"I'm talking about the cabrones he hired to go after her, the ones he sent to scare her away so she couldn't cause any trouble or embarrass anybody. The ones that cornered her in church and said they would cut her throat if she didn't pack up and go back to Mexico."

"Is Josefina safe?"

"From you and your boss, yes."

David knew it would be futile trying to locate her without Huero's cooperation.

"I know what you're thinking," Huero said. "Send those guys in here and we'll cut their balls off and feed them to the dogs. Tell that to the Senator. And tell him that if we don't get what we asked for, his balls are next."

"What exactly is it that you want?"

David detested the fecklessness of his question, but it was all he could think of. To gain any leverage, he had to get as much information as possible. Whether he liked it or not, it was his role to act as the go-between, the missing link. If either Huero or the Senator was going to get his way, he would have to negotiate through him. It made a twisted sort of sense. After all, he not only understood both sides, he *was* both sides. And that duality, dormant for so many years, had left a fissure in his soul. Now the gap had cracked open, leaving him clinging to the sheer walls of the self. David knew that the rational thing to do was to walk out of that garage and onto the first plane back to New York. No sane person would blame him; this was not his problem. But something stopped him from turning away—from his past, from his present, from himself. He certainly wasn't staying in L.A. for Senator Randall's sake. It was a lot tougher for him to accept the fact that Kurt had used him, deceived him, set him up like one of his political pawns. Still, something else was keeping him there in that garage, listening to Huero like one of the Senator's lackeys. He told himself it was pride, or the chance to back up easy talk with action, the possibility of making a difference. But the simple truth was that for the first time in his life he was sticking his neck out for somebody else.

"You already know what I want," Huero was saying. "I gave you a list of the things that need to be done, things that should have been done a long time ago. It's high time for the politicians to start putting their money where their big mouths are."

"And what about the M-1 boys? What's to stop you from pulling another stunt after Josefina's been vindicated? How does the Senator know he can trust you?"

"He doesn't," Huero said matter-of-factly.

"There's something else I need to know," David said. "What's in this for you? What do you hope to accomplish?"

Huero was leaning against the Camaro, arms folded across his chest. He wore his arrogance like a suit of armor. "Justice," he said.

"And what if the Senator refuses your deal? How much justice would be served by bringing down someone who is at least trying to help your people? How would putting a conservative in his place make things better? Is that something you want on your conscience?"

"*Conscience,*" Huero scoffed. "You sound like that damned nun, Sister What's-her-face."

"Ramona?"

"That's the one." Huero spat on the floor, wiping his mouth with the back of his hand. "Conscience is a luxury that can be afforded only by priests and politicians, the dreamers and speechmakers. Me, I'm a pragmatist. I save myself and the ones around me. The rest can go to hell."

"Are you here to volunteer for Senator Randall's campaign?"

She was petite and cover-girl cute, probably still in college. Her hair was pulled back into a neat ponytail, and only a RE-ELECT RANDALL button marred the convex outline of her chest.

"No, I'm here to see his son, Kurt Randall."

An involuntary twitch crossed her lips and David wondered whether she had volunteered her honor to his friend after some late-night fund-raiser.

"Right through here," the girl instructed. "To the end of the hall and turn right."

David thanked her and began navigating the buzzing swamp of cardboard boxes, ringing phones, posters, pamphlets, and assorted election paraphernalia.

Kurt was bent over a Möbius strip of computer printouts, making notes with a blunt pencil. "Welcome to Randall headquarters," he said to David. "What do you think?"

"Very democratic."

"I want you to see something." Kurt pointed to a circled row of numbers. "The latest polls are putting us twenty points ahead of the competition in the minority districts. It's not as much as we hoped for, but it's still a substantial lead."

"Terrific. Kurt, we need to talk."

"It's even higher around East L.A. I thought you'd . . ."

"Now." David said it loud enough to turn a couple of heads in their direction.

"Okay, okay," Kurt said. "Keep your shirt on. The conference room is empty. We can talk in there."

He led David to a paneled room furnished with an oval table and folding chairs. On the blackboard behind the table, someone had scrawled: *Victory is sweet, but defeat is tasteless.* The whole place had a temporary feel about it, like a traveling circus that might fold up and disappear overnight.

"What's on your mind?" Kurt asked after he had shut the door.

"You lied."

"About what?"

"About Josefina being pregnant. About her claiming your father raped her."

"Did she tell you that?"

"Huero did."

Kurt shook his head disdainfully. It was certainly not the reaction David had expected. When Kurt spoke he sounded like a doctor trying to soothe an hysterical patient.

"Now let me get this straight. You talked to him but not to her. And he told you she was pregnant. First off, since when are pachuco gang leaders trained in gynecology? I don't know, maybe she is and maybe she isn't. But if he's accusing my father, then I can assure you that Huero was the one doing the lying. It's just another part of his whole blackmail scam."

"Why didn't you tell me from the beginning, Kurt? We talked about trust, remember?"

"I know. I'm sorry. You've got to understand, my father was already upset enough and there was no pressing reason to tell you. Look, I never thought you'd get far enough to actually talk to Huero. I've got to hand it to you, you're a real sleuth, pal. Believe me, I'm sorry I ever got you mixed up in this. It was a mistake. I'll handle it from here on."

"What about Huero?"

"We'll figure something out. He could still be bluffing. Those guys are capable of anything. They're desperate hombres."

"Desperate enough to have Josefina roughed up to keep her mouth shut?"

This time Kurt was visibly shaken. He closed his eyes and sighed, pressing his shoulders flat against the wall. "My father panicked after the first phone call from Huero. He thought she could be scared into dropping her accusations."

"So he hired a couple of thugs to do the job for him."

"David, don't be so goddamned melodramatic, for Christ's sake. They were some guys my father knew from his labor days. It was just a ploy to fake her out, to put the fear of God into her."

"But the plan backfired."

"That's the understatement of the century."

David was still furious, but confronting Kurt had drained all the fight out of him. He dropped into one of the chairs, suddenly very tired. "None of this makes much sense to me," he said finally, "but let's go over it once more. Just for my own peace of mind, which, by the way, is deteriorating by the second."

Kurt gave him a dejected look, but didn't contradict him.

"Okay," David continued. "One: Josefina disappears from your dad's house with some important papers. Two: your dad's men try to scare her out of town, but end up sending her into Huero's arms. Three: your dad gets a ransom call from Huero, who says he's protecting Josefina, who may or may not be pregnant. I'll give your father the benefit of the doubt for the time being. In any case, you find yourself needing to locate Josefina and maybe strike a deal before she and Huero go to the newspapers with their story. So, four: you call your old buddy in New York and invite him out for a little R&R at everyone's expense."

"I told you, I'm sorry. It's over." Kurt had slumped down the wall into a half-squatting position.

"No, Kurt. It's not over."

"David, listen to me . . ."

"I've finished listening to you, Kurt. I think it's time I have a talk with your dad. He could probably use some legal advice."

"No." Kurt's voice was hoarse. "He thinks I'm taking care of this alone. David, it's taken me years to get close to my father again. You have no right to fuck that up, even after what's happened."

David looked at his friend, who seemed to have shrunk inside his clothes, and his heart went out to him. Besides, there remained the possibility that he was telling the truth. "All right," David allowed. "How you deal with your dad is your business. But then you'll have to tell him that you've made a deal with Huero."

Kurt's head jerked up in surprise.

"The offer is as follows: In exchange for Huero's silence, your dad forks over five grand and a green card for Josefina —think of it as an employee severance package. After the election, provided he wins, of course, your dad does his best to fulfill the list of demands in good faith. That's it, take it or leave it."

"Whose side are you on?" Kurt said.

David saw the wounded look in his friend's eyes and had to struggle to keep his voice steady. "I don't know anymore."

David's hand was shaking as he put the key into the ignition and started the engine. He drove automatically, hardly seeing the road as he steered the car onto the Hollywood westbound and joined the rush-hour flow of traffic. Kurt's last words were still echoing in his ears. He felt both traitor and betrayed, an accomplice in his own undoing, a co-saboteur of his closest friendship. A car tried to cut in front of him, and David blasted his horn. He punched the gas and changed lanes, needing room to breathe, space to think. The setting sun oozed through the evening haze like a punctured egg yolk, bathing the commuters in iodine light. Josefina was very clear to him in the gathering dusk, her head bent in prayer, her face gently lit by flickering candles. How did it happen? Did they drag her from the church by force, or did they politely ask her to step outside? Did they call her a spic or a whore? Did they touch her?

David swerved into the next lane and yanked the wheel, thankful for the raised bumps on the road dividers.

And what about Huero? Did he rescue her like a hero from the pages of her novellas? Had he held her close, made love to her? Where was she now? Sleeping in his bed? Or, more likely, living with his family like an adopted sister, passing the afternoons knitting with his mother, gossiping about the old country, helping with the cooking? David's mind seethed. If Huero had saved Josefina from her assailants, then why did he wait so long to call the Senator? Was Kurt still lying? Was Huero? Round and round the questions went, like Little Black Sambo's tigers, until they had whipped themselves into a yellow blur of nonsense. And above it all, like a dark cloud, was the revolting image of Kurt's father forcing himself on Josefina. David closed his eyes to dispel the thought and then opened them again, just in time to slam on the brakes and brace himself for the impact.

David stared ahead through the windshield, amazed to be alive. Several cars were arranged helter-skelter across the fast lanes, two of them contorted into modern sculpture. One of them had crushed the lower half of a man's body, which was visible on the pavement. A few feet away, a bloody arm dangled through a shattered window. The scene remained in suspended animation for what seemed like hours; only the smell of charred vinyl and the faraway screech of tires denoted the passage of time. A woman's sobbing rose from somewhere in the wreckage. "Call an ambulance," somebody yelled. David's first impulse was to drive away from the carnage. He had been nanoseconds from death, had glimpsed his own mutilated corpse among the victims. He wanted to get away from the agony, find a bar, have a stiff drink, try to forget the sickening crunch of buckling metal. Instead, he ran to a call box a few yards away on the shoulder. He did his best to describe his location and then hurried back to the accident. By this time, a few other people had stopped to help. A young couple, their clothes soaked with blood, sat on the center divider holding hands. David went to the man on the pavement and felt for his pulse. "The bastard cut right in front of me," the man gasped. "I think I'm going to die. Do you know what the scariest part is? . . ." David lowered his head to listen, but the rest of the man's words were drowned out by sirens. David felt something trickle down his hand and realized that he must have scraped his arm on the dashboard. He wiped the blood away with his sleeve, waiting for pain but experiencing only a growing numbness.

It is touted as a free rock concert in the park, a chance to hear some music in the sun. But after the bands finish, the audience stays, as if knowing that the real show is yet to come. It was only a few days ago that the Hispanic reporter from the *Times* was shot in an East L.A. bar. There is a consensus in the community that a line has been crossed, and the tension is palpable as small knots of people stand together waiting, shouting.

A man in jeans and a tank top has commandeered the stage. "Look around you and remember. See us here together and never forget that we are powerful enough to make a difference!" The speaker points to the policemen positioned around the parameter of the field. "Those pigs in the trees know what I'm talking about. That's why they're afraid to show their stinking white faces!"

Cheers and jeers.

"Let them see that even without guns we are a hundred times braver, a hundred times stronger!"

Louder. "VIVA LA RAZA!" Five hundred fists rend the air with a roar of affirmation.

The cops stand by their cars, reflecting the demonstrators in their mirrored sunglasses, cattle ranchers in black and white. Their presence dares the crowd to make a move. It is a paradox of law enforcement that is lost on the officers, but not the organizers, who have used it like a magnifying glass to pinpoint the aimless frustration and resentment.

"Who owns this city? Us or the pigs?!"

"VIVA! VIVA!"

An ominous groan wells up from the crowd as officials disconnect the microphone.

David is there with Mondo and Johnny and a few of the others. They have come to hear some tunes and check out the action, as Mondo put it. Like everyone else, they have stuck around to see if anything would happen, and it looks as if something will. Mondo is standing on a trash can, shirtless, a red bandanna tied around his head. When he raises his arms and shouts, he looks like an Indian brave on the warpath. David stands back, watching with growing apprehension as the crowd begins to flex its muscle. He knows that clenched fists and slogans are not the answer, that mindless action is an expression not of strength but of weakness. He knows that in the long run civil disobedience will only hurt the cause by undermining their credibility.

He knows, too, that to say any of this would mark him as a traitor, a defector to the other side, an enemy of the people.

"VIVA LA RAZA!"

A cherry bomb explodes a hundred feet from polished black boots.

More cheers.

A bottle is hurled like a grenade, shattering the peace into a thousand fragments.

An amplified voice, metallic and inhuman, slices through the air: *Under authority of the Sheriff of the County of Los Angeles, this has been declared an unlawful assembly. Those who do not disperse immediately will be subject to arrest.*

The order is answered with hoots of defiance and a hail of rocks.

"VIVA! VIVA!"

"Let's get out of here," David says, but it's too late. The crunch of a billy club is followed by a woman's bloody cry: "You fucking fascists!"

Plumes of tear gas sprout on the lawn, giving the riot a festive atmosphere as truculence disintegrates into chaos.

More cherry bombs. Screams. Fear. The herd begins to stampede away from the fighting. Friends and family scatter. No one stops running until they are safe; no one is safe until they stop.

David sees an opening in the trees and makes a break for it. A boy about two or three years younger than David follows his lead. Their common goal is a chain-link fence and, beyond that, a row of back yards where they can hide, disappear. Two officers see what they're doing and try to cut them off. David has a longer stride and the boy falls behind. "Wait up," he calls to David, who reaches the fence just as the cops close in. Lifting himself to the top, David straddles the fence and hesitates. Then, calculating his chances, he jumps. As he lands on the sidewalk, their eyes lock through the wire mesh. "Why didn't you help me?" the boy's expression says. But there is no time to answer—there *is* no answer—because the officers have grabbed him from behind and David is running. He runs as fast as he can. He doesn't look back.

Traffic had begun to flow around the accident. Through the windows of the passing cars, David saw the occupants with their mouths agape, transfixed by fear and relief. The ambulance arrived; a tow truck pulled one of the wrecks over to the roadside. The pavement gleamed with spilled fluids. An officer laid a hand on David's shoulder. "Go home," he said. "There's nothing more you can do." David watched a body being lifted away. The fumes and flashing lights brought tears to his eyes, but no feeling.

7

"Happy birthday, Grandma."

"Mijito!" she exclaimed, clutching him to her withered breast like a lover.

She hadn't expected to see him again so soon.

David looked at the deep lines in her face and saw the ravages of a lifetime that had spanned wealth and penury, a civil war, and the sorrow of a husband who was already slipping into senility. There was an unfamiliar sweetness on her breath and a feverish light in her eyes. David guessed she had been drinking.

"Here, Grandma, this is for you," he said, taking out a package from under his arm.

"Gracias, mijito. Thank you."

Over her shoulder David could see the rest of the family straining to get a glimpse of the little boy who had become such a stranger.

"Pase, mijito. Come in."

David nodded to the faces around him, most of which he no longer recognized. It was always like this whenever he came home. He felt awkward and he wished his mother were there to smooth things over. He held out the package.

"Open it, Grandma."

There were murmurs in the room as she fumbled with the heavy wrapping. He knew the old women were talking about him, scrutinizing his every gesture like a geriatric jury. After an eternity the wrapping lay in a heap on the floor and she lifted up the bundle of yellow cashmere.

"It's a sweater, Grandma," he explained needlessly.

"Muchas gracias, mijito. Es muy beautiful."

She posed like a model, her hand lifted coquettishly to her ear. The audience of old hens clucked in approval.

David ducked into the den, where an assortment of nephews and nieces were watching TV in the dark. The glow from the screen turned their faces blue, and David imagined their minds and souls permeated by the same dull monochrome. The commercial ended and a movie came on. A voluptuous woman clad in animal skins was running through the forest.

"Hey, that's Raquel Welch," David said.

"Who's Raquel Welch?" the girls asked.

In the kitchen, a clutch of adults were engaged in a lively game of lotería. It was a variation of bingo played with sectioned boards and a deck of cards depicting ordinary objects like a rose or a horse. Pennies marked the squares that corresponded to the cards drawn from the deck. It was a game of chance, yet the images on the boards gave the game symbolic resonance. He stood in the doorway and watched as the cards were turned over with the hushed reverence of a Tarot reading.

The horse . . . The black man . . . The tree . . .

A woman started screaming and flapping her arms like a bird that was too heavy to fly. "I've got it, I've got it," she bellowed. The center of the table was quickly covered by a heap of coins, and she pulled them toward her with greedy relish. "I'm really rich now," she gloated. A few of the players looked at each other and laughed.

"Hey, tiger." David felt the impact of a heavy hand slapping his back. It was his Uncle Raymond, the liquor-store owner and commercial kingpin of the family. Whatever the occasion, Raymond would invariably show up barking orders

134

to young clerks laden with cheap booze and beer. He also tended to be his own best customer. "Where have you been hiding all these years?"

David extended his hand, a gesture that his uncle parried with a rebuke.

"What's this? No abrazo for your old Uncle Raymond? Are you too important to hug your own blood?" David extricated himself from Raymond's bearlike embrace.

"Is the good life in New York making you soft?" he joked, jabbing his nephew in the ribs.

"Nope," David replied, trying to stay out of range of his stubby fists.

"So tell me, how much is my big-shot nephew making these days?"

"Enough."

"How much is that? Sixty? Seventy grand?"

"Something like that."

Raymond took a playful swing at David, who lurched back, knocking a plastic cup off the kitchen counter.

The jousting match had gone on as long as David could remember, even when he was a child and Raymond would tease him for not throwing the ball higher, for not being tougher, for not showing his anger. They were on stage now and everyone in the room was enjoying the spectacle. Even the lotería game had halted. Someone mentioned how much taller he had gotten.

"Well, that's pretty good money around this cow town, but I bet it's chicken feed in New York. Am I right?"

"Always, Ray."

There was a commotion in the living room as David's mother and father made their entrance. It would take them a while to finish exchanging hugs and hellos.

"You're still a smart-ass," Raymond concluded, reaching out to cuff him on the ear but jabbing into space, because David had been fast enough to pull away.

It sounded like a radio playing in the back yard. Except

that the highs were too rich and the bass parts too natural to be emanating from speakers. David realized they were real guitars, real voices. The song was a gentle ballad with a robust melody that David recognized as "Las mañanitas." The musicians were seated together in a corner of the patio, and the listeners had arranged their chairs in a semicircle amid the trees and potted plants that thrived under his grandmother's nurturing attention.

The birthday girl was seated with the band, joining in the chorus with lusty abandon. Her hair was tied up in a blue ribbon, and David caught a fleeting image of the beautiful young woman she must once have been. Others joined in, and soon everyone there was singing, some with eyes closed, retreating into a secret place of dreams and memories too fragile to survive in the bright sunlight. Afterward, the notes seemed to linger like spiderwebs clinging to the breeze.

David's parents had been listening, too.

"She's drunk again," Ernesto said with dismay. "She'll fall and break her hip."

"It's her birthday," Susanna admonished. "She can have a few drinks if she wants. Hi, mijo." She kissed her son on the cheek and rolled her eyes toward her husband.

The musicians were playing again. This time the strumming was vigorous and joyful. David's grandmother took another swig from her glass and started clapping her hands in time to the bounding rhythm.

"Vamos a bailar," she announced, and was answered by whistles and cheers.

"She's going to hurt herself."

"Leave her alone, Ernesto."

Raising her skirt above her ankles, she began to dance. She moved gracefully in small, strutting steps, her heels kicking to the beat. A few of the men took turns as her partner until she pushed them away with a laugh.

"Venga, mijito," she called to David.

"C'mon! Dance with your grandma!" they all cried.

One of the women grabbed him by the arm and pushed him onto the patio. His grandmother swirled her skirt and David did his best to follow along, tripping on his own feet like a fumbling schoolboy. Then David took her in his arms and they were suddenly in sync, twirling together on the cement to raucous applause.

"Mijito," she whispered, holding him closer. And for a split second they were alone, spinning in a circle of timeless movement. David sensed they were falling long before it happened. "Un milagro, a miracle," the old women muttered, but David knew better. It was not God but the chair that had slowed their descent, giving him a chance to twist around and take the brunt of the impact. The fall had only knocked the wind out of her. As for David, his ribs would heal much faster than the wound that opened when his father struck him.

"You could have killed her," he yelled, drawing back for another punch. But Susanna was already between them, screaming, "No, leave him alone! Hit me first, Ernesto. Hit me!"

"Go ahead," David heard himself saying. "Hit her. Hit me. Kill us all, you stupid old man. Just like you almost killed Johnny."

"You disrespectful . . ."

"There's nothing left to respect."

"Shut your mouth before I break it!"

David wanted to say more, but someone had put a hand over his mouth. His father's body was shaking with rage as the other men led him away.

Alone on the patio, David sat staring down at an ant trapped between his loafers. The insect tried in vain to circumvent the enormous barrier made by his shoes, until it stopped in its tracks, paralyzed with panic. David looked up again at his grandmother's garden, and it occurred to him that her hands, so much like withered roots, would soon be returning to the soil. He dusted off his pants and went into the house to say goodbye. She was lying quietly on her bed, her new sweater still draped around her shoulders.

"Grandma, I have to go," he said, taking her hand in his. The gentle pressure from her fingers said that she understood, that she didn't blame him for what had happened or would happen. But it was the resignation in her face that told him something in both of them had died that day.

David's eyes wandered over the room, resting on a photograph on the dresser. The frame was dusty but the picture sharp. His grandmother is posing with both hands on the handle of an old-fashioned water pump. Despite being soaking wet, she beams at the camera with unbridled contentment and humor. They are on a family vacation at his aunt's house in Texas. David is barely eight or nine when they arrive at Uncle Carl's ranch. His grandmother and her sister Aunt Rosa have gone outside to draw water from the well, where the mutual excitement of their reunion incites a splashing contest. When David runs out to join the fun, they let him have it with a bucketful. He expects the water to be warm, but it's bracing cold, and his consternation must show, because they start to laugh. The shock of the dunking combined with being the butt of their joke is more than he can take and David starts to cry. He knows he must be a hilariously pathetic sight: a big strong boy bawling over some spilled water. But David doesn't care. All that matters is the indelible image of the two women as they come forward to comfort him, their wet locks clinging to their clothes like black rope, their faces tilted into the sun, laughing.

"I knew you'd be back," Sister Ramona said as she opened the door and let him in. David was surprised to see her wearing jeans and a loose white blouse. Her hair was cropped short, but the way it curled around her forehead and ears made it seem more chic than severe.

"You look a lot better out of uniform."

"Thanks," she said, acknowledging the secular implications of his compliment. "We don't wear habits to look sexy. We wear them to show our devotion to God."

"I realize that. I'm sorry."

"Don't be sorry, Mr. Loya." She reached for a Marlboro. "You didn't come here to discuss ecclesiastical couture."

"No, I didn't."

"So?" She took a deep puff and exhaled.

"I thought I knew. But now I'm not so sure."

Sister Ramona looked skeptical. "Have you found Josefina?" she asked.

"No. I mean, I think she's with Huero, but he won't let me see her. He could be lying."

"He's not lying," she said firmly.

David waited for her to continue, but she remained impassive. "When I talked to him he mentioned your name. I didn't think you two would know each other."

Sister Ramona stubbed out her cigarette. David was sure she was going to ask him to leave. Instead, she coughed and leaned forward. "Mr. Loya."

"David."

"David," she repeated with the stern patience of a teacher indulging her pupil. "All I know about you is that you are a liar and that you're looking for Josefina Juárez. Now, unless you take me for a complete fool, which would be a mistake, I assure you, you can't expect me to tell you anything unless you first tell me the real reason you're here."

David told her everything except the Senator's name.

Sister Ramona lit another Marlboro, and David followed the pale ribbons of smoke.

"If you no longer care what happens to your friend's father," she said finally, "then why don't you just go back to New York?"

"Josefina's been deserted by enough people," David said. "I've been having dreams . . ."

David tried to regain his composure. He had no intention

of breaking down in front of a nun. That's what psychiatrists were for.

"You're a Catholic?" she asked.

"Technically."

"When was the last time you had Holy Communion?"

"Look," David said more harshly than he meant to, "I didn't come here for a Sunday-school refresher course. We made a deal. Now it's your turn to tell the truth."

Sister Ramona seemed to be sizing him up. He thought he saw a flicker of sexual appraisal in her gaze, but suppressed the idea. He had enough on his mind without adding fantasies about having sex with a nun. "How do I know you can really help Josefina?" she asked him. "Even if your intentions are good, what makes you think you can change anything?"

"Do you have a better offer?"

"May God have mercy on us all," Sister Ramona said, and the wall between them lowered another notch. "She came here to pray, for hours sometimes. We were friends, or least I was somebody she could talk to. A few weeks ago I sensed something was wrong. I asked her about it and she said she was pregnant. I had to respect her decision not to tell me who the father was. About a week later, she showed up at my door in hysterics. She told me that some men had followed her and threatened to kill her if she didn't go back to Mexico right away. Of course, she wouldn't go to the police. She was afraid to stay, afraid to leave. I did what I could to console her."

Sister Ramona took another puff. "Not too long after that I was working late in the classroom when I heard screams coming from the courtyard. She was curled up in a ball, trying to protect her stomach. Two men were standing over her, punching and kicking, calling her names. I yelled and they ran off. I wanted to phone the police, get her to a hospital, but she wouldn't let me. I helped her to get home, made her some tea. We prayed together. When I got up to leave, she said, 'I'm going to lose the baby. I can feel it dying inside me.' "

"Jesus," David said, covering his face with his hands.

Sister Ramona looked surprised.

"You didn't know?"

"No."

Sister Ramona waited a moment before resuming her story. "I saw her again about a week ago. I knew she had left her apartment and was under Huero's protection. It was obvious she had had a miscarriage. I tried to get her to a hospital again, but she wouldn't hear of it. She seemed to blame herself for what had happened. She was very upset. That was the last time I saw her. I say the Rosary for her every night, praying that the Virgin will look after her."

"Somebody's got to get through to her," David said. "Huero can't hide her forever."

"If he wouldn't let you see her before, what makes you think he will now?"

"When I relayed Huero's demands, I added one more: that Josefina would get papers and enough money to start a new life."

Sister Ramona had begun to pray. Creases of concentration formed on her forehead as she recited the sacred litany.

"What good is that going to do?" The words were like dust in David's mouth. "We've seen how the Lord rewards the faithful. Where was God when Josefina called Him?"

As David rose to leave, Sister Ramona looked at him with something akin to pity. "I'm not praying for Josefina," she said quietly. "I'm praying for you."

Even in the gathering gloom of dusk, it didn't take David very long to find his way back to Huero's garage. The cars had been moved and the heavy metal door had been pulled down and locked. David got out of the car and followed a narrow alley around the side of the building. Through the barred windows David could see figures moving in the light of a single bare bulb. David went through to the front of the garage and pounded on the door. A dog started barking across the street and David turned in time to see a hand pull down a window shade. David knocked again, and this time he heard the sound of approaching footsteps.

"Talk to me," a voice ordered.

"I need to see Huero."

There was the clang of bolts being thrown back and then a loud scrape as the door was lifted open.

"What do you want, motherfucker?" David recognized the acne-pitted face of one of Huero's guards.

"I need to talk to Huero. It's important."

"Visiting hours are over, man."

"I need to see him tonight," David insisted. "At least tell me where I can find him. It's important."

The guard hesitated.

"He's going to be pretty pissed off when he finds out you blew the deal for him," David warned.

"He might be here later tonight."

"Then I'll wait until he shows," David said, pushing past him. He waited for a hand to grab his shoulder. Instead, he heard the door slam shut. David was aware of the man following him as he walked toward the light at the back of the room. There were two guys David hadn't seen before: one stocky and long-haired; the other tall, with a scrawny goatee. David caught the pungent aroma of marijuana and something else he couldn't place. A radio on the tool bench was tuned to a Mexican station. The music was a norteño corrido, the vocalist warbling over a bubbly polka beat. David translated the words in his head:

> *I never had the nerve to say I love you*

*And now you've gone and left this
    town
So instead I'll kiss the stars above you
And hope your heart will come
    around.*

The Camaro Huero had been working on was gone, and
in its place stood a wooden bench and a few vinyl chairs.

"Where'd you find the maricón, Angel?" the fat one asked.

"He wants to talk to Huero again. He says it's important."

"Are you a narc, man?" the fatso growled.

"No."

"That's good," he said. "Real good for you. Because if you
were a narc, we'd have to kill your ass." The fat man's belly
quivered in amusement.

"Light the pipe, Homes," Acne-face said, rubbing his hands
on his thighs.

"Sit down, dude," Angel said to David. "Relax."

He took the chair next to him, but Angel remained standing.

Fatso was aiming a butane lighter into a small glass pipe.
He took a hit and passed it on. When the pipe had circled
back to Fatso, he turned to David. "You want some of this
shit, maricón?"

"No, thanks."

"No, thanks?" he repeated, pretending to be offended.
"Doesn't he know anything about Mexican customs? It's
not polite to refuse an offer from your host. Heavens to
Murgatroyd, that's very rude." He looked over David's shoulder. "Maybe we have to teach this vato some manners, eh?"

Fatso loaded another chunk of brownish crystal into the
pipe and leaned closer. As David started to stand up, he felt
something cold and sharp against his neck.

"You'd better be careful, mano," Angel warned. "You might
cut yourself."

Fatso's face filled David's vision as he held the pipe to

143

David's mouth. He tried to turn away and felt the tip of the blade penetrate his skin.

"Move again and you'll be breathing through your Adam's apple," Angel warned.

"Just take it in your mouth and suck," said Fatso. "You know how to do that, don't you, maricón?"

David could hear Acne-face's wheezing laugh as he took a small puff. The acrid smoke burned his lungs and he started to cough, already feeling the rush.

"That's better," Fatso said. "Now do it again."

David felt the blade move against his neck and took another lungful. This time his scalp tingled with electricity. The room seemed to constrict until there was nothing in it but the knife at his neck, the pipe, and Fatso's face.

"More," he ordered.

"What the hell's going down here?"

It was Huero. At least it was Huero's voice; the tone and arrogant slouch belonged to Mondo. As David peered at the figure in the shadows, it became increasingly difficult to make the distinction. Then there was none.

"We were just helping this dude relax while he waited for you," Angel explained, replacing the blade in his pocket.

"Get away from him," Huero barked, and the command was instantly obeyed. "You know I don't like you using that shit."

The light behind him projected his oversized shadow on the wall. "Loya, what the fuck are you doing here?"

David gingerly touched his neck and felt a stickiness on his collar. "Your friends are a bunch of sadistic pigs," he said.

"You should talk, compadre." The words were dipped in venom. "Why are you here?"

David forced himself to be lucid. "I need to talk to you about Josefina."

"Then do it," Huero snapped.

Maybe it was the effect of the drug, but Huero seemed a

changed man from their first encounter. The confident general of the day before had been replaced by an edgy dictator. David saw the knotted muscles in Huero's jaw and his skin crawled. A drop of sweat inched down his back.

"I found out about the baby from Sister Ramona," David said, trying to focus his thoughts. "The Senator accepted your deal. She'll get papers and enough money to start over. I know you're an honorable man. Let me take her to a hospital."

"So that's why you came back," Huero said. "To tell the wetback you tried to kill that she can move to the suburbs. Like those gringas who get dishpan hands in the commercials. Naturally. Why else would you be here?"

Huero made a monkey face and scratched the top of his head. "I must be a dumb Mexican, Loya. Because I never believe one word of the bullshit that comes out of your mouth."

David almost giggled. It was the drug. His heart thumped in his chest, pumping tainted blood into his brain. As long as it lasted, he knew he could stand up to Huero. Synthetic confidence was better than none at all. "You have no choice, Huero. Take me to Josefina or there's no deal."

"You just want to talk to Josefina."

"Let me see her or the deal is off."

Huero began to pace, his hands clasped behind his back. He was the philosopher-statesman again. "I guess that's not asking too much," he sneered, "considering how much you two have in common."

David ignored Huero's jibe and tried to keep his mind clear. The most important thing was to get through to Josefina. He knew she had every right to hate him, but maybe he could make her understand. If anyone was capable of forgiveness, it was she.

"Yeah, why not?" Huero was saying. "But there's one condition: you have to wear a blindfold. I can't let you see where we're going, can I?"

David suppressed a stab of panic. He was about to give up the last vestige of his control over the situation. "Whatever you say."

A folded bandanna was placed over his eyes and pulled tight. He could hear the chairs being moved and Huero giving orders. Someone grabbed him by the arm and moved him in the direction of other footsteps. The damp night air licked his cheeks and arms. He had heard these sounds, felt these things before. It was like finding a neglected part of a house, or sorting through a box of discarded clothes. Did they still fit? Maybe he should try them on. A leather jacket. A white T-shirt. His old sneakers. Time to hit the street, go for a cruise.

His surroundings became a fluid mosaic of dislocated sensations: The muffled slam of car doors . . . the slightly industrial odor of tuck 'n' roll seat covers . . . an engine clearing its throat . . . the sizzle of a match igniting . . . the sweet stench of marijuana . . . Right about now someone usually turned on the radio . . . There it is, a fickle hand adjusting the tuner: snippets of rock, disco, an announcer saying, "But that's not half as bad as" . . . a woman's voice wrapped around a plaintive guitar . . . "Hey, leave that on, man. I like that song" . . . David always rode shotgun when he wasn't behind the wheel; he only let Mondo drive when he was too loaded to do it himself . . . "Turn here" . . . Mondo liked the power of being behind the wheel. Maybe too much; David had awoken one night after a beach party to find him pushing a hundred on the freeway . . . "Hey, make sure Loya is okay; I don't want him ODing on us" . . . a hand nudging him . . . "Lay off, Mondo" . . . laughter . . . laughing at him? . . . Nobody could burn rubber like Mondo, that was for sure . . . "Man, look at the slicks on that one!" . . . They were at an intersection . . . the clamor of traffic, a honking horn . . . "Watch out for the pigs" . . . They were moving again . . . The window was open, hair whipping in his face . . . "Take a left here. That's it. Help him out" . . . Hands on him again.

146

The scrape of shoes on the sidewalk . . . his shoes . . . the crunch of an unlucky snail . . . "Fucking babosos. I hate those things!" . . . Shoes on cement steps . . . a creaking screen door . . . stuffy warmth . . . hot tortillas on the stove . . . a baby crying . . . "Hey, what's in the fridge? Check it out" . . . His mother always left him something to nibble when he came in, she didn't think her boy should go to bed hungry . . . "Let me have some of that, man" . . . It didn't matter what time it was, as long as he came home . . . Footsteps on linoleum . . . "This way" . . . quieter now . . . whispers in Spanish . . . a bedroom? . . . a door being closed . . . a woman's perfume . . . breathing . . . heartbeats . . .

Someone else was in the room with him.

"Josefina?" David reached up to remove the blindfold.

"Leave it on." A woman's voice.

Then a slender hand touching his face, moving down to his neck, shoulders, chest. A jolt of desire shot up his spine. She pressed against him and he could feel her breasts through his shirt. His wildest fantasy coming true? He knew it couldn't be even before the blindfold was torn from his eyes.

"You sick bastards."

It was just a tease, a cruel joke at David's expense. Huero and a couple of the others had been in the room all along, watching the tawdry passion play. Now they were making fun of him. The girl laughed, too, but not without a trace of regret.

"No," Huero corrected. "You are the sick bastard. You and the oppressors who treat our women like whores, who take what doesn't belong to them."

Huero ran his fingers through the girl's hair.

"You wanted her, didn't you? It was obvious, my friend. Don't be ashamed; Becky's a real turn-on. But she belongs to me, and you'll never have her, just like you'll never have Josefina either. No matter what happens, you'll never be able to hurt her again. That's one of the lessons you'll learn to-night."

They were in a windowless room with a mattress on the floor. A Bible and some dog-eared novellas were on the night-stand. A poster of the Virgin was taped to the wall next to the closet. David knew he was in Josefina's room.

"What have you done with her?"

Huero turned his back and David lunged. They took him easily, holding him down until he agreed to quit struggling. David tasted bile with his defeat, and it suddenly occurred to him that he might never leave the room alive.

"Where is she?" David demanded again.

"She is someplace where you will never reach her."

David looked at Huero as if he had never seen him before.

"Do you believe in God?" Huero asked, holding the Bible in his hands like a preacher giving a sermon. "Josefina did."

Huero's expression became distant. "She was very religious, you know. I tried to tell her that God and the devil both lived in men. I tried to tell her that only other men could defeat the devil, but she wouldn't listen. 'The Virgin will protect me,' she told me. And maybe for a while it was true. Heaven and earth are not so far apart, you know."

He followed David's gaze to the poster of the Virgin.

"Take the Virgin, for instance." Huero turned and pointed to the image like a professor referring to a map or chart. "Did you know that a few years ago a group of respected scientists did some studies on that picture—not *that* picture, of course; the original on that cloth they keep in Mexico—and they came up with some very interesting stuff. You see, they used X-rays and computers and carbon dating and all that shit, and decided that the image on the peasant's coat was gen-uine. Then they did something even more amazing. They used high-powered microscopes to enlarge the Virgin's pup-ils to study something called the Purkinje-Sanson effect. What that means is that the pupil of the human eye—yours and mine, too—supposedly reflects the images that are in front of it. In other words, if you look close enough at a picture of an eye, you can see what was in the room when the picture was taken."

148

Huero turned to his audience. "Amazing, eh? I didn't know that either. Anyway, they did that to the picture of the Virgin. And you know what they found in the Virgin's eyes? Can you guess? No? I'll tell you. They found the images of the Bishop and the peasant Juan Diego, just like the legend of the miracle says. Think about it! The miracle is right there in the Virgin's eyes, like a ghost left to haunt the rational mind. It's really fantastic. So you see, science and religion are not opposed the way some people say. One truth does not replace the other truth. They go hand in hand."

"Why are you telling me all this?"

Huero's smile was candid and self-mocking. "I went to college, you know. I even taught some high school. So I can recognize intelligence in another person. I could have been like you if I had wanted to. I could have crossed the line and never turned back. You and me, we're not so different, really. We're brothers under the skin."

He registered David's incomprehension. "Not the brown skin that others see," Huero explained. "The layer just below it. The skin we live in."

The earth below David's feet shifted, and it took him a moment to regain his balance. He felt the depressing letdown of the ebbing crack high and realized he was finally sobering up.

"That's why I quit teaching," Huero was saying. "I realized that I was actually telling my kids to put on somebody else's skin, a skin that could never stretch enough to fit them."

"Are you going to tell me what happened?"

"To Josefina?"

"Yes."

Huero's face became gaunt. It was the first time David had seen him show any sign of weakness or compassion. What other facets of feeling were obscured by the macho exterior? There were no doubt many Hueros: Huero the professor, Huero the cynical preacher, Huero the revolutionary, Huero the gangleader. Maybe even Huero the true believer.

"I told you that she thought the Virgin would protect her,"

he began. "She almost had me believing it, too. Her faith was very strong. But the evil she encountered in this world was even stronger. She never had a chance. First they took away her honor, then her child, then her will to live. Maybe the car that hit her didn't really hurt her. How can I say that? Because by the time she walked into the street she was already crippled inside."

Huero came closer and regarded David with genuine puzzlement. "Why are you crying, Loya?" he asked. "I thought this news would make you happy. Now you can go tell your masters that their problem has been solved by an old lady in a Buick who was so blind she thought she had hit a dog. You and I know that dogs don't wear dresses, don't we? But this stupid old lady"—Huero pointed to his head—"couldn't grasp the concept. Randall can finish his steak dinner in peace and light up a fat cigar afterward to celebrate. Talk to me. Why are you sad, hombre?"

Huero couldn't resist a last twist of the knife. "Do you love her or something?"

But the answer remained unborn in the depths of David's despair, a place that up till now had remained hidden and safely locked away. He repeated Huero's question to himself until the words became strange and unutterable, like a foreign language that he was only beginning to learn.

8

In movies and dreams hospitals are always white, but this one was painted a moldy shade of green. Nurses and doctors flowed through the corridors, clotted in groups of two or three in front of doorways and along counters made of textureless Formica. They were mostly young and healthy and seemed preoccupied not with disease and death but with each other and the results of the Dodgers' doubleheader. As he passed a row of occupied rooms, David couldn't resist spying. A few plastic tubes and blinking machines notwithstanding, they might have been cut-rate rooms at the Holiday Inn. The patients were engaged in the same things they would be doing in a hotel at this hour—reading or sleeping or vacantly watching TV, making plans they might or might not get to fulfill, rearranging their itineraries. Every surface shone. David looked for pain or fear in the faces and found only the telltale signs of boredom and wordless exasperation. The worst thing about hospitals, he decided, was the way that they conspired to make death unexceptional, drained of ritual and mystery.

At the end of a brightly lit hallway, a woman with thick glasses presided over a stack of clipboards.

"I'm looking for a girl who was admitted here sometime yesterday . . ."

"Name?"

"Josefina Juárez. She was hit by a car."

The woman looked up from her papers. "Are you a relative?"

"Her brother."

"Wait here, please, Mr. Juárez."

The woman furtively ducked behind a labyrinth of file cabinets. David felt like a criminal. What if they asked to see some I.D.? The woman was probably calling the police right now, promising to keep him there until they arrived. He watched the procession of white and green uniforms marching like color-coded insects; hurrying in one direction, then another, excitedly intercepting each other, single-mindedly moving on.

Then David was seized by a terrible anxiety. What if Josefina wasn't really hurt? What if this was just another joke?

The woman reappeared and handed him a form to fill out. Her suspicious glances only intensified his unease as he gave a phony address and telephone number. Where it asked for Josefina's profession, he wrote "Tourist."

The woman squinted at the clipboard. "We need you to identify the body, Mr. Juárez. Sign here, please."

"The body?"

Her frown disappeared. "I'm sorry," she said. "I thought you already knew."

A half hour later, an orderly led David to the elevators. One of the man's shoes squeaked and David had the notion that this somehow made him unfit for dealings with the dead, let alone their bereaved relatives. When they reached the basement, David had an irrational urge to ask him to take off his shoe or hop on one foot. But he held his tongue, even when, in an effort to break the ice, the man said, "You're lucky she's still here. Unidentifieds are usually sent to the county morgue right off the bat."

They entered another corridor, one without counters or potted flowers or cheery Muzak. No one who passed them smiled, and the air was laced with the stench of formaldehyde. At least death was respected down here in the basement, where the limits of modern medicine were dissected and catalogued for future reference. Underground, the public pretense of scientific infallibility all but disappeared, and in its place David almost welcomed the grim reassurance of the bottom line.

Double glass doors were pushed aside to reveal a brightly lit vault filled with rows of sheathed bodies. The only ordinary furniture in the room was a gray metal desk with a small sticker on the top drawer that read: THE BUCK REALLY STOPS HERE. Beside the typewriter, a half-eaten orange glistened obscenely in the stark fluorescent light. The orderly glanced at the papers in his hand and motioned for David to follow. He methodically sorted through the plastic tags affixed to the cadavers until he found the right one.

"The listed cause of death was internal injuries," he said in a nervous tenor. "You can request an autopsy from the hospital at your own expense."

"That won't be necessary," David said.

The orderly took hold of the plastic sheet and turned to David. "Ah, sometimes, sir, ah, people have a little trouble dealing with this part. If you start to feel ill or anything, just let me know. It's perfectly normal under the circumstances."

"Thanks," David said, realizing that the man was really a boy, an intern who was paying his dues with the lowliest job in the hospital. "I'll let you know."

The intern gingerly pulled the sheet down past Josefina's face and kept going, until David could see the beginning of the tuft of black pubic hair.

"That's far enough," David said.

"We need a positive I.D. from a family member before the body can be released."

She was not as pale as he had expected; the brown cast of her skin was faded but far from colorless. Her breasts were firm and well shaped, her waist narrow. She was even prettier than he had remembered from the photograph, certainly pretty enough to rekindle the lust in a middle-aged man who perhaps found himself alone one afternoon in the house with one of his employees. A young girl whose defenselessness was not only physical but social and legal as well. David couldn't tear his eyes away from her body, her large dark nipples and full lips now the color of dried roses. More than anything else he felt cheated. There were so many questions he wanted to ask her, there was so much they could have taught each other. It had taken David thirty years and three thousand miles to find her, and at the last moment she had eluded him. It would no longer suffice to accept what had happened as a random succession of unfortunate events. The odds were infinitesimal, and besides, David did not believe in gambling. No, this was high tragedy, and such stories always had a moral, a message from the Fates. He impulsively reached out to touch her slightly parted lips. What was she trying to tell him in death that she could not say to him alive? Why had God gone out of His way to mock him? If she were still alive, what would she want him to do?

The intern stared at him with growing alarm and took a step forward. Without thinking, David shoved him back from the table.

"Why don't you buy a fucking decent pair of shoes," he said.

The old woman expertly mashed the coarse dough in her palms, pulling off pieces the size of a golf ball and slapping them into thick round patties. With a quick twist of her wrist she let them fall onto the grill in a movement so fluid it seemed like an act of nature. Her unbound hair was the color of burning charcoal—dull black dusted with gray— and it fell across her broad Indian features like a shadow. When the tortilla was lightly charred on one side, she deftly lifted it off the fire with her fingertips and cradled it in her left hand, stuffing the trough of masa with strips of braised beef, minced tomatoes, chopped onion, salsa, and cilantro.

"Two dollars, please," she said, handing the taco to a blond adolescent in pink surfer jams.

The woman looked at David. "Taco, mister?"

"No, gracias. I'm waiting for somebody."

The woman shrugged and turned her attention to the man in the next stall, who was busy dipping candlewicks into a vat of melted tallow.

David looked at his watch and began retracing his steps toward the beginning of Olvera Street, hardly hearing the mariachi band that entertained a gaggle of Izod-clad tourists. David remembered the first time he had ever been there, during a fifth-grade field trip to "the oldest street in the city of Los Angeles." His teachers seemed to think it was wonderful that the Spanish flavor of Old California had been preserved in the center of a twentieth-century megalopolis. He was sure they had spouted something about "Mexican-American roots" and the importance of "ethnic history." Now, as David looked at the rows of high-priced Indian handicraft stores and health-food burrito stands, he saw only a monument to commercialized culture. How ironic that the founding site of the city should be turned into a freakish museum, complete with friendly natives who sold their dignity a piece at a time by trafficking in "authentic" trinkets and "hacienda-made" treats.

She was waiting for him in front of the souvenir shop, impatiently fingering a miniature straw burro.

"Marta?" David asked.

"Hi," she answered, holding out her hand. "I can't stay long. I've got a class later this afternoon. I'm taking English at the college."

She saw the consternation on his face and drew back. "Is something wrong, Mr. Loya?"

"No, of course not. It's just that you're so different from what I expected. Would you like to sit down?"

"Yes, thank you."

Marta was wearing a crisp cotton blouse set off by a navy-blue skirt and black pumps. Her hair was pulled back into a smart bun, enhancing her high cheekbones, long lashes, and caramel complexion. All that, along with her American accent and body language, made her seem like an assimilated version of Josefina.

"I only came because Sister Ramona said you were a friend," she said after ordering a Coke, and David noticed Marta had not completely overcome the tendency of Mexican women to avoid looking men in the eye. "And to help Josefina, of course. How is she?"

"I'm sorry to be the one to tell you this. She's dead."

"Madre de Dios," Marta whispered, reverting back to Spanish for a moment. She crossed herself, then reached for her purse and pulled out a handkerchief. "What happened?"

"It was an accident," David said. "She was crossing the street when a car hit her."

Marta dabbed at her eyes, the smudged mascara leaving dark splotches on her cheeks. "How awful. I can't believe it."

"Do you know a person named Huero?"

"He didn't do it." The conviction in her voice surprised him.

"You know him?"

She shook her head.

"Then how do you know?"

Marta didn't answer. David waited for her to calm down again.

"I'm trying to find out more about the time before she disappeared. How did you two become friends? Especially since, well . . ."

"Since we're so different?" she asked, finishing his sentence for him. "I've been in the U.S. two years. One year already when Josefina came to work for Senator Randall. She was a lot like me when I first arrived. I tried to help her, you know, to teach her things. I knew what it was like to come here alone and be treated like dirt, with no one even to talk to."

She paused, as if mentally correcting her grammar. "Of course, I didn't have the Virgin to talk to. God forgive me, but that was her big problem."

"Her problem?"

"I mean that Josefina," Marta strained for the right words, "that girl was living in the past. She was not bad-looking, you know. I tried to get her to go out, but she wouldn't even think of dating a man. Everything was a sin to her. She never went out, she didn't try to learn English. Me, I came here to be an American. If I wanted to be a Mexican, I would have stayed in Mexico. No sir. I came here and met Freddie. We're going to be married."

"Congratulations."

Marta was suddenly self-conscious again, as if she had been indiscreet by talking so much about herself. Was it real shyness or an act? There was a shrewdness in her manner that he couldn't help admiring. Like Josefina she had come with nothing. But unlike her friend, she had adapted quickly to her new home, found herself a man, reinvented herself. A survivor.

"I'm sorry," Marta said. "It's just that that's why at first I was happy when it happened. I thought, Well, at least she's normal like the rest of us poor sinners."

"When what happened, Marta?"

She blushed. This time it was real.

"Listen," Marta gave a furtive glance at the tables around them. "I can't be involved in anything. I'm still not legal until I get married. It's dangerous for me."

"Don't worry," David said, trying to reassure himself as much as anyone. "No one is going to find out about this conversation. I'm a friend. Please. This could be very important."

The band was strolling in their direction, and David had to lean forward to hear over the blaring horns.

"She had been acting, you know, funny," Marta went on. "It was not like her, but I didn't think too much about it. Then one night before I moved—I was living at a place not too far away, you see, before I moved in with my boyfriend—I went by her house to invite her to the movies. You know, the Mexican movies in Spanish. It was the only thing she liked to do except for praying. Anyway, I went by that night to see if she wanted to go and I saw the Cadillac parked across the street. That's how I knew."

"Whose Cadillac, Marta?"

"Senator Randall's."

There was a smattering of applause as the mariachis finished their set and passed around the sombrero.

"I'm sorry. I'm late for my class," Marta announced.

"Wait."

"That's all I can say. Por favor. Don't try to find me again."

He watched her hurry into the weekend crowd, pushing past the taco lady and the candle man, until she disappeared completely into the swarming riot of color.

The rays of the Lord's Day were glinting on the Hollywood sign as David drove back to Santa Monica. The air was unusually fresh and he had a clear view of the Bay and the rugged blond cliffs that stretched north toward Malibu. Seagulls wheeled in salute to the morning and the Pacific shimmered like liquid silver. There was no question about it: Balboa's ocean was bluer than the Atlantic. For all its beauty, the East Coast remained painted in his mind in shades of brown and teal, turquoise and pale green. Only the Pacific could become this shade of sapphire, so lambent and pure.

There was no sign of Kurt at the apartment. Despite his having been up for nearly forty-eight hours straight, David was wide awake. He changed into his trunks and went outside. Except for a lone jogger and a few surfers bobbing out on the swells, the beach was deserted. David stood on the edge of the shore watching the hypnotic roll of the waves, letting the pristine foam envelop his toes before retreating into the wash. He began to wade in, slowly, deliberately. He yielded to the insistent tug of the surf until he was submerged up to his hips; then, as a breaker reared above him, he dove in and felt its pounding weight slide over his shoulders and back. The inevitable tightness in his chest threatened to engulf him, choke him, but he refused to let it. Water was all around him now, gently massaging his limbs, speaking to him in the primal alphabet of ebb and flow. For a few precious seconds there was no up and down, no past and future, no right and wrong; only the surging, irresistible force of the sea. At that instant it became the only thing in the universe that mattered—that and the promise of his next breath. David felt his feet brush the sandy bottom and pushed off. He came up gasping for air, trying to swallow the sky. He filled his lungs with oxygen and dove again, this time deeper, and drowned the last vestiges of his fear before allowing himself to float up and shatter the translucent surface.

Kurt was waiting for him on the steps of the deck when he got back to the house. He was in a crumpled suit sans shirt, his arms folded parallel to the weathered railing. As he came closer, David saw the fatigue on his friend's face and felt a pang of regret for what was about to happen.

"Nothing like an afternoon dip to get your blood moving," Kurt said, trying to stifle a yawn.

"You should try it sometime."

"Yeah, but why go and spoil a perfectly good hangover?" Kurt picked up a fistful of sand and let it run through his fingers.

"My mistake," David allowed. "Spent the night out, eh?"

"She found politics fascinating."

"So you gave her the old party line."

"Yeah, right." Kurt let out a halfhearted laugh. "But I didn't tell her who to vote for."

"Oh, right. I forgot how ethical you politico boys are."

"You know what they say at ringside"—Kurt was doing Howard Cosell—"May the best man win."

"No matter who gets hurt." David avoided Kurt's stare.

A seagull hovered overhead, squawked, and disappeared over the house.

This was the wrong way to do it; they were talking in ciphers. The least they could do was be straight with each other. He owed Kurt that much. But how do you tell your best friend that his father is a murderer?

"Since when did you get so moralistic?" Kurt said over his shoulder, but David had already turned his back to go inside. He felt grimy and wanted to rinse off before this went any further. He pulled off his trunks and climbed under the shower. He adjusted the knobs until the temperature was almost hot enough to hurt, then switched over to bracing cold. David stayed that way for a long time, watching the oversized droplets stream off his nose and splash on the drain. Then he got out, toweled, and looked at himself naked in the mirror. He saw a thirty-year-old man with the Nautilized body of a middle-class professional. A man who had been variously mistaken as Indian, French, Italian, and Spanish. A man who had been born in the barrio and educated at Harvard, a stereotype of upward mobility. Toweling his face, David looked at his reflection in the mirror and wondered what color he was.

Kurt was sitting on the couch staring blankly at the television set when David re-entered the living room. On the screen, Napoleon Solo had just entered a basement laundry and suavely made his way to a closet in the rear. He hit a hidden switch and the wall swung back to reveal the secret headquarters of the United Network Command for Law and Enforcement . . .

"I thought we had a deal," Kurt said flatly.

"The deal's off," David answered. "Josefina's dead."

Buzzers and blinking lights signaled that an intruder had penetrated the U.N.C.L.E. complex.

"What?" Kurt sounded more annoyed than surprised.

"Those guys your father sent to rough her up turned out to be real pros. Funny thing, it turns out she really was pregnant, after all. When she lost the baby she lost everything. Even the sense not to look both ways before crossing. They had to pry her out from under a car."

The intruder was firing his gun at Solo, only to have the rounds stopped by bulletproof glass. Solo took a quick step to the side and cut down the killer without even mussing his hair. Solo and Illya Kuryakin exchanged knowing glances.

"I guess I should have expected it," David said, growing angrier. "I don't know why I thought you'd give a shit. Maybe you won't give a shit either when this whole mess shows up in the papers."

"That guy is a double-dealing con artist," Kurt said as he clicked the set off. "Without the girl, no one will believe a word Huero says."

"Maybe not, but they'll believe me."

Kurt swiveled his head around. "And what," he said, "would be the point of that?"

"She never stole any papers, did she, Kurt? There never were any papers."

Kurt sighed. "That hardly makes any difference anymore, does it?"

"It does to me."

A dim smile of recognition crossed Kurt's lips, then dissolved. "It was the only way to make sure you'd help. A moral incentive, if you will. But it's no reason to jump to conclusions about . . ."

"A woman was raped and now she's dead, Kurt. It's not a rumor, it's not a ploy. I saw the body a few hours ago. What the hell's happened to you? Have you gone nuts? Look at me, damn it. She wasn't nothing. She wasn't another computerized campaign statistic. She was a human being." David gave Kurt a chance to respond before delivering his next sentence. "Somebody's got to pay."

"And you think it should be my father."

"It was his fault, Kurt."

"No, it wasn't." His voice sounded tinny, as if it was coming from the other end of a long tunnel. "I already told you that."

David shook his head. "I found Marta, Kurt. She saw your dad's car parked in front of Josefina's house."

"Marta saw my dad at Josefina's house?" Kurt asked harshly.

"She saw his Cadillac."

"Come on, man. Are you kidding me? Do you know how many Cadillacs there are in Los Angeles? I told you already, those people are all in cahoots together."

"That's one party line I never bought, Kurt. And after everything that's happened . . ."

"What exactly *has* happened?" Kurt was up on his feet. He leaned his arms on the table opposite David, his mouth contorted into an ugly grimace. "What laws have been broken, Counselor? Your accusations of rape and murder would be laughed out of any court in the state. If my father wasn't a well-known politician, this story wouldn't even rate a paragraph on the back page, and you know it."

It was true. It seemed that no matter how certain he became about anything, five minutes with Kurt and he was vacillating. Kurt was pacing with his head bent in concentration, the parody of a defense lawyer having his big day in court. He was doing Perry Mason, and it was a bravura performance.

"Let's assume," Kurt intoned, "for the sake of argument, that what your little barrio friend said is true about my dad being the father. But let's take it from another angle—same facts, same outcome, different perspective. In this scenario, a Mexican girl, pretty, penniless, and all alone in the big old U.S.A., comes to Los Angeles. To what? To become an American, or to make a little money, or maybe both. She gets a job changing the sheets of a successful politician. She works hard. She's got a pleasant personality. She's trusted, accepted into the household. Her boss is dashing, powerful, and famous for trying to help her people in his own limited way. The attraction is natural. At first the affair is totally platonic, kind of *Father Knows Best* meets *La Bamba* . . ."

David started to protest, but Kurt raised his hand.

". . . I know, it's a bit too prime-time, but please be patient with me. Like I said, they're close, but not too close for comfort. Until one fateful night when Josefina works late and misses her bus. It's after dark and you don't have to be the Shadow to know what lurks in the heart of the metropolitan transit system. The good Senator's been home for a while; he's had a few martinis, maybe even a few too many. But being the considerate boss, he offers to drive the poor girl home. She demurs, of course, he insists, they take the Cadillac. During the ride they have a nice chat, thanks mainly to the Senator's high-school Spanish and a bit of old-fashioned body language. The Senator has been around the block enough to know when a woman is coming on to him. And this, as far as he can tell, is exactly what she is doing in her coy Latino way. Needless to say, he ends up walking her to the door of her shabby little flat. It's dark and the Senator feels anonymous, transported even, certainly safe from the prying eyes of Beverly Hills socialites with big tits and mouths to match. In short, they kiss. They kiss harder. Fade to black."

"Who directed this movie, Kurt?"

"Please, please hold your reviews until the last reel. The Senator goes home and knows he has done a bad thing; he knows it in his head and heart and promises himself not to take advantage of the help again. Under normal—and I admittedly use the term loosely—circumstances, this would be The End. But this is a modern romance and the fun has just begun. Because on Monday morning, our heroine shows up bright and early for work and head over heels in love.

Unfortunately for all concerned, the girl's got good taste but bad judgment. The Senator gives her the cold shoulder and she goes to pieces. Then she discovers that she is with child and the shit hits the fan at the Randall residence. He fires her. But she starts showing up in public places, reminding him that he's the father. To make matters worse, it turns out she's a wetback to boot. Meanwhile, there's an election to be won and appearances to keep up. The Senator sees his whole career going down the tubes for a single night's indiscretion. Ergo, he freaks and calls the dogs out to scare her away. Instead, they send her into the waiting arms of the local pachuco warlord. Before you can say Viva Zapata, the Senator gets a phone call from Huero, the blackmailing bandito, who tells him to steek 'em up or else. At wit's end, the Senator decides to confide in the only person he can trust: his son."

Kurt raised his hand again, signaling that he was nearly finished. He spoke in a tone of heartfelt sincerity, as if delivering his final summary to the jury. "Now, before you say anything, think about this tragic story, pal. Search your conscience a minute and ask yourself if what happened makes the Senator an evil man, a man who deserves to be destroyed to avenge the death of a girl who was on a kamikaze course right from the beginning, who may or may not have brought all this bad news upon herself, but who certainly was not above using deception, extortion, and political blackmail during her misguided lunge for the big brass ring in the land of the free."

A slender shaft of sunlight formed a luminous line across the table. David knew the line was inside him, too, sundering his mind and heart along with his loyalty to Kurt. The line had finally become visible to David, and it took every iota of his strength to cross it.

"It doesn't make him evil, Kurt. Just guilty."

Kurt took a step forward. "You can't do it, David."

"Why not?" David asked, bracing himself.

"Because it would be a mistake, and you're too smart not to know it. Even if my dad was the villain you make him out to be, you'd still be wrong. It's ludicrous, really. I mean, you hang out with your long-lost cousins for a few days and all of a sudden you've discovered your roots like some kind of Chicano Alex Haley. It's like those middle-class blacks who go on safari to get in touch with their ancestors. I've seen it happen, David. The natives, the real Africans, take one look at their jive soul brothers from Watts and all they see are American tourists with bucks to spend."

Kurt was practically pleading. He held his hand out for David to shake. "No matter what those Raza rebels told you, you aren't one of them and you never can be," Kurt said, his voice growing firm. "You're a fucking Harvard grad, for Christ's sake! You're American, not Mexican. David, you're one of us."

David looked at Kurt's outstretched hand and willed himself not to take it. "If killing innocent people is what it takes to be one of us, you can count me out of the club."

Kurt's hand dropped.

"I know what you're saying, Kurt," David said, struggling to speak over the static roaring in his ears. "And maybe there's some truth there. But I can't go along with it, not this time."

"So what are you waiting for," Kurt said, his voice like lead. "The phone's right over there."

David knew that if he didn't do it now, it would never happen. He moved to the phone and lifted the receiver, wishing that a bomb would drop or the world would end before he had a chance to dial the number. David knew it by heart; he had started to call so many times over the past two days that the digits were branded into his memory.

"Max Rogers on the City Desk, please. Yes, I'll hold."

"Remember that week we spent on the Cape," Kurt said. He was sitting again, his arms folded around his legs like a kid who had broken a toy or lost his parents at the zoo.

"Yeah, sure I do."

"You swore then that you'd back me up no matter what."

"I know I did, Kurt."

"You know that story I just told you, about what happened with Josefina?"

"What about it?"

"It wasn't my father. It was me."

"Hello?" Max's voice came on the line.

David bit his tongue until he tasted blood mixing with his saliva. Then he swallowed and hung up.

The Cape is everything Kurt promised it would be. They have been there less than a week and already David cannot imagine ever having lived any other way, any other place. They spend their days toasting their limbs on the wide sandy beach, reading Kafka and Kerouac, sleeping off their hangovers and scoping girls at what Kurt calls "the preppie spawning grounds." Despite his initial reservations, David has been seduced by the limpid days and misty nights, the cheesy roadside cornucopias of plaster frogs and spinning whirligigs, the chinos and Top-Siders, the blue-collar bars and weathered mansions. Kurt's parents have rented a house near the marina for the summer, but this week they are in Europe and the boys have the whole place to themselves. They have brought along some homework with the pretext of getting it done, but the books remain stacked in the corner, untouched.

They talk about everything—from the worst symptoms of bubonic plague to the best episodes of *M*A*S*H*, from the closing battles of World War I to the most sure-fire opening lines—anything but law. They drink beer for breakfast and skip dinner, preferring to chow down on the hors d'oeuvres that are so unstintingly proffered along the evening cocktail circuit. They bask in the youthful luxury of looking and feeling good. Long hours in the sun have put white streaks in Kurt's hair; David's deepened bronze provides a dashing contrast to the white sports jacket he has purloined from his friend's closet. David is constantly amazed by the number of people Kurt seems to know, how many attractive girls they meet every day. They stumble home each night with silly grins on their faces and scribbled phone numbers stuffed into their pockets. One night they double-dated their way to adjoining bedrooms, although Kurt's date, a loquacious brunette from Vassar, was unwilling to go the whole nine yards. Everybody here seems to have gone to school with somebody else's brother or mother or son, and at times David thinks the entire East Coast social scene is one enormous Spring Break.

Tonight's soiree is being held at the preserved colonial owned by a retired admiral known for his collection of antique wooden duck decoys. David picks one up and almost drops it when Kurt tells him how much it is worth. On principle, David bets Kurt ten dollars that it won't float, and the boys sneak into a bathroom and put one in the toilet to verify its buoyancy. It lists until its beak is dipping below the waterline but does not sink. Trying to keep a straight face, David balks on the basis that the toilet water is not salty like a real marsh. In the interest of scientific rigor, Kurt opens his fly and makes as if to piss on the duck just as an elderly lady barges in. "Nobody here but us woodpeckers," Kurt yells at the quickly closing door, as they stifle paroxysms of laughter.

Sometime later, David finds himself pinned to the wall by a matron who is hell-bent on rationalizing the history of U.S. policy in Central America. "Where would the freedom-loving majority be if we had never supported the Contras in Nicaragua?" she is saying. "Probably Miami," David answers, the whole time tracking the movements of a black-haired beauty in a blue chiffon dress. Long-limbed and vivacious, she is like a dark flower surrounded by a buzzing swarm of men. He has tried, but can't even get close enough to catch her eye. Across the room, Kurt is pointing his thumb at the door and David nods that he's ready to make an escape.

Five minutes later, he and Kurt are watching the moon set over the bay as they tread home along the water's edge.

"Who was the vision in blue?"

"You are developing a very refined taste for poontang," Kurt answers sardonically.

"Just tell me."

"I beg your pardon; I didn't know you were betrothed to her. Her father is on the federal appellate court. Jennifer Lansing. We're talking major bucks, major tits." Ellipses hang in the air, drift away. "Hey! What's the only thing better than pulling a rabbit out of my hat?"

"You're not wearing a hat."

"Don't distract me, my boy." Kurt is doing W. C. Fields now. He reaches into his jacket and holds up a bottle of mescal like a trophy.

"Jesus, Kurt. I can't believe you did that."

"Anyone who has the balls to stock a bottle of this in his bar is asking for trouble, amigo. Those old farts probably don't even know what this is. I mean, this stuff is dangerous! One whiff and the old girls would be humping their crystal doorknobs. Not to mention what would happen when they noticed the pickled larvae floating around inside. I tell you, we deserve a medal. Probably saved their reputations and their marriages. Maybe even their lives!"

"You are so full of shit," David says gravely, but he is smiling.

"Think so, eh? It just so happens that mescal was invented in Mexico by your ancestors—the conquistadors—after they ran out of their own liquor stash. It's made from the agave plant, which the Aztecs used to make pulque, which, I'm sure your grammy has told you, is the world's oldest booze."

Kurt is on one of his legendary rolls. Snake charmer, dime-store philosopher, Shavian wit, and Good Old Boy all rolled into his wiry frame, ideas and emotions rippling across his features like a satellite weather map. There is no stopping him when he is like this, not that anyone would want to try. Part of his charm stems from this ability to conjure up the moment and serve it back to the participants. Spontaneity and instinct take over. Anything is possible so long as it furthers the cause of fun and friendship. Kurt is leaning against a small dune, the bottle nestled between his legs like a talisman. With a ceremonial flourish, he breaks open the seal and unscrews the cap.

Kurt's head is tilted at a jaunty angle as he speaks. "It is a well-known mixological fact that anyone who eats the worm will have visions, hallucinations, and an all-expenses-paid trip to meet the great mixologist of the universe."

He takes a healthy swig and holds the bottle out to David, who makes sure the worm doesn't come anywhere near his mouth as he drinks. The crude cactus liquor burns his throat like acid. He hates the taste but understands the importance of masculine ritual. Sharing a stolen bottle of mescal on the beach is something only the best of friends would do, and David feels honored.

"So tell me about the girl," David persists.

"What girl?"

"The one in the blue dress."

"Oh, right." Kurt acts as though they are discussing ancient history. "First, take another drink."

David drops to his knees and tilts the bottle up to his lips like a trumpet player. Kurt lets out a hoot of approval, throws a rock at a crab scuttling over the dune. David can feel the stored heat of the day in the sand beneath him. The tinkle of boat rigging is carried to them by the breeze, and to David it sounds more beautiful than any symphony.

"She goes to Vassar, has more money than brains, and still collects dolls."

"It doesn't really matter. Either way she's out of my league."

"How can you say that?" Kurt belches and passes the bottle again.

As David drinks, he sees the worm spinning in a corkscrew of lazy circles. "Because it's obvious. I mean, I can't keep up with a girl like that. If my name was Kennedy, maybe."

"That's the biggest crock of bullshit I have ever heard. David, listen to me." His friend's hand clamps onto his shoulder. "You're wrong, pal. I know. I've dated that type of rich bitch, and I can assure you that underneath their trust-fund façades they are a bunch of spiritual peasants."

Kurt digs his fingers into David's shoulder, as if trying to physically drive in his point. "In fact, I know you are a better person. I hold you in higher esteem than all those rich, pampered assholes. Than myself even."

"You're inebriated," David says matter-of-factly.

"No, I'm not. I mean, yes, I am, but I'm still making sense. Hell . . . Stop interrupting me. You, my friend, have nothing to lose. Most of these people's sole purpose in life is to hold on to what they've got. That makes them vulnerable and afraid of anything new. That fear kills something inside. They become materialist zombies trapped in velvet coffins, only able to come out at night, when they attend charity balls and suck the blood of young virgins . . ."

He punctuated the sentence with a hiccup.

"Now I *know* you're drunk," David scoffs.

Far from offended, Kurt is incredulous at his friend's denseness. "Don't you see? They, those people, just *think* they're somebody."

"And I just think I'm nobody."

"*Au contraire, mon ami.* Just the opposite. Because you can be *anybody.*"

Before David can answer, Kurt is vertical again. "See that rowboat out there?" He is pointing to a skiff anchored a couple of hundred feet from the shore. "I'll race you there and back."

"You're crazy if you think . . ." But Kurt is already shucking off his clothes.

Yodeling like a madman, Kurt reaches the bay and plunges in with an exaggerated splash. Laughing, David watches, hesitates, follows. The water is clammy and dense as he immerses his ankles, now the rest of him. David has never been a particularly strong swimmer, and with every stroke Kurt widens his lead. The moon is down, but David can hear Kurt somewhere ahead in the darkness. He points himself in the same direction and tries to swim faster. A swell catches him in the face, filling his mouth. David gags, catches his breath. There is a slowly spinning whirlpool in his head, a mescal and saltwater cocktail that threatens to engulf him. He somehow regains his stroke as he spots the outline of the boat, a patch of deeper black against an indigo background. Kurt is standing on the deck, yelling, "C'mon, you slack ass!" David gets there gasping and too disoriented to do anything but cling to the gunwale. He hears another splash behind him and realizes that Kurt has already started back. David wants to stay with the boat, but he's too cold and too afraid to remain out there all alone. He has a fleeting glimpse of himself from somewhere far above: a shivering speck of flesh adrift in the nocturnal void. Fighting back another wave of nausea, he lets go of the boat. Up ahead, behind the dunes, the lights from the elegant bay windows shine like a beacon. They seem far away, impossibly beyond his reach. His arms are like weights as he struggles to keep his head up. He thinks he hears Kurt shouting, but his ears are filled with the sounds of rushing water and his thumping heart. Thirty feet from dry land, the cramps set in and he imbibes more of the bay. Panic grips him like a swift current, carries him down under the opaque ripples. I'm drowning, he thinks, I'm going to die and become food for the crabs. The bay seems to be clutching at him the way a person would. It's got him by his arms and neck. He tries to fight it, but it's no use, because it's stronger than he is.

It's still night when David opens his eyes. He knows because he can see the Little Dipper and a thousand other stars that he never learned to name.

"Shade, you all right? You had me a little worried there for a minute."

Kurt is kneeling beside him in the sand, drying his face off with his shirt. David just looks at him, looks at the sky. He feels unspeakably close to the stars; they seem to be shining for his benefit. David remains motionless, afraid to break the spell of knowing that his best friend has just saved his life. He knows better than to try to put his emotions into words; it is part of their code to express intense feelings with nothing more than an ironic look, a glancing blow in the shoulder, a joke. There is no need to sully their friendship with the corny conventions of ordinary sentiment. They are above that sort of thing. Much better to silently savor the moment and then set it free, never letting it touch the ground.

"Flash."

"What, Shade?" Kurt answers, leaning closer.

"Who won?"

"Hey, mister. Over here!" the boys shouted. David intercepted the ball, bounced it a couple of times on the pavement before throwing it back too hard. As it sailed over their heads, one of the boys slapped his forehead with his fist in a comic gesture of exasperation. David had almost forgotten what it was like to be around a schoolyard full of children at play. The beleaguered adults were shouting and waving their hands in a losing battle to maintain order.

David focused on a little girl playing jump rope with her friends. Her braids flew in the air as the rope slapped the ground.

"Uno. Dos. Tres. Quatro. Cinco . . ."

She cringed in mortification as the rope snagged her foot.

"Muy bien," David called out, and the girl smiled back before running off.

David turned and climbed the steps to the church. Inside, the din from the schoolyard was barely audible and David detected the circumspect sounds of worship. He went directly to the shrine of the Virgin and knelt down before the gilded statue. David dropped a quarter into the collection box and lit a candle. Then he stuffed in a whole dollar and lit four more.

"You're either very generous or very repentant."

It was Sister Ramona. He couldn't help noticing the pink and green Swatch adorning her wrist.

"Maybe neither."

The nun shook her head in mild reproof. "Still walking the line, I see."

"Not really." David straightened up. "I was coming to see you, actually. I have some bad news."

"About Josefina? I already know. The funeral is tomorrow. Thank you, David."

"For what?"

"For doing your best. I know what happened with Huero, and later at the hospital."

"It wasn't enough, was it?"

"That isn't for us to decide." Sister Ramona turned to look at the Virgin. "If you have a minute later on, maybe we could share a cup of coffee."

"I'd like that," David said.

"See you in a few minutes, then."

After Sister Ramona had left, David looked up again at the robed image. The Virgin's expression remained inscrutable, hinting at some ineffable sadness. Was she grieving for Josefina and the countless thousands like her? David now knew for a fact that God was not all-powerful; He was bound by an infinite chain of pain and sorrow. David still wasn't sure if heaven existed, but there was no question about hell. That was one part of the Church's teachings he could accept without qualification.

Looking at the statue again, David remembered what Huero

had told him about the Virgin's eyes. If only he could see through them long enough to look upon the world with such equanimity. What had Josefina seen in the Virgin's gentle features? Hope or pain? Suffering or joy? Maybe all of those things, maybe something more. Would she have agreed with Huero about heaven and earth being closer than anyone suspected?

He rose to his feet and walked down the side aisle, halting before three narrow doors. Velvet curtains were drawn across two of them. David entered the third. He could hear the priest murmuring absolution on the other side. In a few seconds it would be his turn. But David wasn't ready yet. He was trying to remember something crucial, a phrase he had once known by heart. The small plastic window slid back and he could see the priest's waiting shadow through the grating. Then, somehow, the words were on David's lips. They had been there all along, safely entombed in his past, waiting for him to need them again.

"Forgive me, Father, for I have sinned."

9

She takes his hand and leads him away from the beach, into the jungle. As they enter the dense canopy of leaves, the sound of crashing waves recedes, replaced by a cacophony of shrieking birdcalls and insects buzzing like high-voltage wires. The air is heavy with pollen and the perfume of a thousand flowers as they follow a narrow clay footpath along the banks of a trickling stream. David peers into the brackish water and sees a school of rainbow-colored fish darting in every direction, like a living kaleidoscope. He wants to stop and show his companion, but she pulls harder on his arm. "Hurry or we'll be late," she says as they continue wending their way into the midday twilight of ferns and hanging vines. David is surprised to see a figure coming toward them on the trail. It is a peasant leading a herd of cattle. The shepherd is wearing coarse cotton clothing, sandals, and a straw hat. In his right hand he carries a staff, which he uses to lead his herd off the trail so that David and Josefina can pass. "Buenos días," David says, hoping to strike up a conversation. "Muy caliente." Thinking the man didn't understand, David illustrates by wiping his brow. But the shepherd only nods, showing a set of protruding teeth. "They won't speak with you," the girl says afterward, but David is too tired to ask why. Just when he is sure they will never leave the jungle, he detects a gentle incline in the landscape. Gradually, the trail disentangles itself from the stream and the vegetation becomes drier. Shafts of sunlight begin to burn through the overgrowth. They emerge at last onto a ridge of sloping hills, a light breeze brushing their hair.

"That's where I was born," Josefina says, pointing to a cluster of whitewashed houses clinging to the edge of a broad plain.

As they descend toward the village, the angle of the land is steep enough to make them run. David trips on some loose rocks and Josefina giggles, dashing for a field of ripe corn. He chases her through the maze of tall green stalks, guided by thrashing leaves and an occasional glimpse of her white dress. The game ends with the two of them rolling in a heap on the moist black earth. David pins her wrists to the ground, and her hair is like an ebony fan behind her head. He kisses her and the quick heat of her response tells him that she wants him.

"No," she says, pushing him off her. "There isn't time."

He begins to protest, but she is already on her feet, heading toward the houses. He starts to laugh, because everything is suddenly so simple. His whole life has been leading him to this exact time and place. A beautiful melody begins to play in his head and David starts to sing along, his voice echoing across the valley. He is perfectly happy with the thought of pursuing Josefina in an endless chase, capturing deeper meaning with every escape.

A highway runs alongside the village, and as David and Josefina walk along the shoulder, a bus full of tourists roars past. Their white faces press up against the windows, looking out with curiosity and revulsion. The shiny camera lenses and sunglasses make them look like giant bugs or alien creatures.

"Vultures," Josefina says.

"Why do you say that?"

"Because anything alive scares them. They are interested only in things that are dead."

The bray of a scruffy burro heralds their arrival in the plaza. The fountain in the center of the square is choked with rust and the larger buildings are veined with jagged cracks. David steps lightly, trying not to kick up the thick dust under their feet. The village seems empty, except for a dog and some chickens, but David senses that they are not alone. Someone moves a curtain in one of the adobe shacks, or is it the wind?

"Wait a minute," David says, suddenly disoriented. "You just spoke English."

"No," she answers. "You spoke Spanish."

They pass a church decorated with pieces of colored tin and plastic flowers. The doors are wide open and David has an urge to go inside, but again Josefina tugs at his hand.

"Where is everyone?" David asks.

"At the ceremony; you'll see."

The last house on the street has a pink curtain instead of a door. Josefina pulls it aside and motions to him to follow. Inside, an old woman greets them. She is dressed in a simple peasant dress and huaraches. She moves with great difficulty, as if in pain. Her olive skin is loose and wrinkled like toasted filo.

"My mother says she is sorry that all we have are beans and tortillas, but she has been ill ever since my father was killed."

"When was that?"

"I was fifteen."

Josefina serves him a simple supper of boiled beans with cilantro and onion in a clay bowl. Suddenly ravenous, David is grateful for the food. The two women watch as he eats.

"We were living in Culiacán," Josefina continues without any prompting. "My father was working for the federal police. My mother always had a new dress to wear, but whenever he went into the jungle, we prayed to God that he would come back to us in one piece. He was usually gone three or four days, and just when we were desperate with worry, he would burst in through the door, drunk and laden with presents like the Three Kings. One day he went out and never came back. My mother and I prayed for three days, asking Jesus to help us find him. The next morning, a farmer who lives near the river appeared at the door and told us that he had seen my father's body floating in the river. We went to the police station and they said they were looking for him, too. They told us that my father had been working for the Federales and that our lives were not worth two pesos. So we left as fast as we could and came here. I wanted to go to Mexico City, but my mother forbade it. She says that in the cities they put poison in the water and the air to kill everyone off so that there will be room for more people."

The old woman slowly nods in confirmation. Her eyes are sunk back in her head like burnt-out sockets.

"How old are you now, Josefina?"

"Seventeen."

"That's impossible."

"Why don't you ask me if you're dreaming?"

"Because I want it to be true."

Josefina blushes, then stands and pats the folds in her dress.

"It's time to go," she announces. "They're waiting for us."

David thanks Josefina's mother for the meal, and she nods goodbye with a feeble smile. Outside again, Josefina leads them toward the road, in the direction that the bus came from.

"Where are we going?"

"There." Josefina is pointing to a cluster of small hills.

"There's nothing there."

"On the other side, in the valley of Mexico."

Time becomes elongated, like looking through the wrong end of a telescope. They mount the hill and start out over a plateau extending as far as he can see. It would take them days to cross, but when David looks down, his feet are not touching the ground. Their progress is totally disproportionate to their speed, but whenever David tries to talk or ques-

178

tion his guide, she holds her hand to his mouth and hushes him. Pointed hills and patches of shimmering water appear in the distance, and after a while David can distinguish human shapes moving on the massive silhouettes. They draw closer and hills are revealed to be pyramids. At first the geometric shapes seem smooth, but then he sees that they are adorned with detailed carvings and hieroglyphics. They come to a bridge that marks the parameter of a vast city. A man wearing feathers and a serpent's head greets them at the gate.

"Five pesos admission, please," he says.

David looks around, but there is no sign of the tourists. He pays the fee and the serpent-man takes them past the guards and into the center of an enormous courtyard. There is some sort of festival going on. Thousands of people are singing and dancing in an orchestrated pattern. It is obviously some sort of celebration, a pageant of some unknown purpose. David is blinded by the procession of gold ornaments and bright costumes. He turns to ask Josefina a question and sees her being led away by the serpent-man. When David tries to follow, the guards block his way.

"Wait for me," she tells him as she disappears behind the pyramid.

"Don't worry, she will come back. They must prepare her."

The words are coming from a wizened old man leaning on a crooked staff. He introduces himself as Matán.

"Chicano?" Matán asks.

"Yes."

"I knew it," Matán says with a sigh. "Qué lástima."

Instead of responding to Matán's insult, David asks, "How long has this city been here?"

"Since before time and after time." Matán waves his arm. "As long as the sun and the moon rule the universe."

David looks up and sees that both celestial bodies are inexplicably sharing a cloudless sky. They loom directly above, impossibly close to each other and to the earth. Matán notes his astonishment and begins to laugh. The sound coming from his mouth is like a dry wind. It occurs to David that everything around them is arranged in perfect symmetry: sun and moon, silver and gold, night and day, male and female. The music and dancing stop and a hush falls over the courtyard. Matán is gone, but his laughter remains. Something important is happening. A shadow flickers across the ground, marking the circular flight of an eagle overhead.

Josefina has returned with the serpent-man. There are painted markings on her cheeks, and glittering ornaments dangle from her ears and neck. Judging from the respectful attention that is given to the serpent-man, David guesses that he must be a shaman or priest. A small group, with Josefina at the center, begins to climb the chiseled steps that lead to the top of the pyramid. David follows, and this time nobody stops him. As the procession ascends toward the altar, David is mesmerized by the glorious panorama of temples and villages extending as far as the sea. They reach the apex, and the transformation of the view is as dramatic as a masterpiece that has at long last been unveiled. Like a blind man suddenly struck with vision, David sees the horizon resting on the pinnacle of the second temple, immutably poised in perfect balance with the heavens. To see better, David closes his eyes. Now he is flying above the ancient city, looking down at thousands of multicolored ants. He tilts his wing and catches a rising draft of wind, thrilled in a mindless rush of upward motion.

Since before time and after time . . .

Scanning the ground for signs of prey, David locates himself still standing atop the pyramid, and only then remembers that he is not a bird.

Human again, David looks at Josefina lying on the polished slab of rock and realizes he is about to lose her a second time. He tries to go to her, but other arms restrain him.

"Don't resist," she says to him. "This is the way it has to be."

An attendant moves forward, hands Matán a bundle, and steps back.

"But I want to stay here with you forever."

Matán opens the cloth wrapping. The obsidian blade gleams in the fierce sunlight.

"You already have."

Josefina's dress is lifted to reveal her swollen belly.

"Then why did you bring me here?"

"So that you could see this and understand."

The black knife slices her flesh from collarbone to navel in one fluid movement, and David's scream is echoed by the cry of the eagle. Rivulets of blood travel down the side of the altar, becoming snakes that slither away on the slippery stones. David is still screaming when Matán reaches his hands into her gaping body, but no one listens. All eyes are on the priest as he chants the sacred words and triumphantly lifts the fetus high into the air.

The couple upstairs were fighting again. David thought it was like tuning in to the sound track of a daytime soap opera. Heavy footsteps. Shouts. The thud of something being thrown against a wall. More shouts, followed by the wet smack of skin on skin. The shrill plea of a woman yelling, "Keep your hands off me!" Footsteps again. Sobbing. The oddly industrial sound of water running through the pipes. Once, during one of their more violent spats, David had seen a flowerpot sailing past the window. Luckily, no one was hurt when it smashed onto the sidewalk below. Later the same day, David ran into the couple in the lobby of the building. They had their arms around each other, cooing like two docile lovebirds.

Not that it was any of David's business. He only gave a damn about the noise, and that had become a moot question. In a few hours he would be leaving New York. Packing it in. Pulling the plug. Jumping ship. He had signed over his lease to a divorcée in her mid-forties from Connecticut who was ready to "spread her wings in the big city," as she put it. David had nodded understandingly and handed her the keys to his old cage.

Like a salesman or rehabilitated convict, he was traveling light; most of his belongings had been put in storage for retrieval at a later date. Possibly much later. David had been only slightly surprised to discover that when it really came down to it, he owned precious little of lasting value. All he was taking with him were a couple of suitcases, some clothes, and a few personal effects. The rest he had bequeathed to friends or left in the trash bin for the sidewalk scavengers.

There was a letter on the coffee table from Sister Ramona thanking him again and asking him to stay in touch. Her missive was uncannily on target, wishing him "the blessing of our merciful Lord and the guidance of the Virgin" on his travels. She had closed with the postscript: "I know Josefina has found peace and that you will find what you seek."

David closed his eyes and tried to imagine Josefina and her baby looking down at the world with the Virgin's weary smile. He held the image in his mind for an instant before letting it dissolve in a haze of disbelief, forever out of reach, impossible to grasp.

He didn't hear the phone until after the third ring.

"It's me," Andrea said. "I got your message."

"Thanks for calling back. I just wanted to say goodbye before I left. I'm not exactly sure when I'll be back."

"You quit the firm?"

"I just ordered them to take a vacation."

He could hear the smile in her voice. "I suppose they got the hint."

"I think so."

Right on cue, the ruckus upstairs halted abruptly, only to be replaced by loud groans and rhythmic thumping.

"Hello? Is something the matter?"

"No. It's just the neighbors making up again."

There was a pause and David felt the question coming before he heard it.

"David, what went wrong? I really thought we were on the right track."

"It's not you who got on the wrong track. It was me."

"I read in the papers about Senator Randall getting re-elected," Andrea said. "That's what you went out there for, isn't it? Were you a consultant for his campaign or something?"

"Not really. I just showed up at the right place at the wrong time, that's all."

"And you're not going to talk about it, are you?"

"There's nothing to say."

"What about Kurt?"

A pause.

"We used to be friends."

"You're not anymore?"

"I don't know. I'm going to have to think about it."

"I give up. You always were a lousy gossip—but a good lay."

Neither of them spoke for a moment. Maybe the time they spent together wasn't such a waste. Maybe those people upstairs could teach him something, after all.

"David, do me a favor. Don't give up so easily."

"I won't."

"Promise?"

"Cross my heart."

Why spoil a happy ending, David thought, and was about to hang up. But that's not how it went; she had something more to tell him.

"I would have married you."

"I know," David said.

"I still don't understand why you're leaving. And why Mexico? You've never been close to your family. You don't even like spicy food."

zing. She could smell the presence of another woman
ife, but how could he ever explain? David gripped the
tighter and made a mental bow to female intuition.
"I guess I thought it was time to develop a taste for it."

"Isn't there another reason?"

She was swinging blindly, hoping to connect with a lucky
punch.

"That's what I'm hoping to find out," he said.

A few minutes later David took a last look at his apartment
and saw nothing more than a practical arrangement of windows, walls, and floors. He was leaving behind no ghosts,
only lint and the unsullied outline of furniture on the walls.

It was better outside: a limpid autumn day, sharp as a
tempered blade. New York never gets better than this, he
thought. There was plenty of time before his flight, so he
left his bags with the elevator man before taking a final stroll
down Fifth Avenue. A leaf floated past him and landed in
the gutter, an early casualty of the approaching winter. David
took it as a good omen: no cursing the snow where he was
going.

The skyline seemed revived by the crisp autumn air, and
he looked at it with reborn appreciation. Maybe he was already someplace else, maybe he never did live here. In that
case, it was altogether fitting that his last minutes in town
would be spent like an incidental tourist's, gaping at the
stores and con artists who lived off the by-products of idle
curiosity. A crowd of people were gawking at something in
front of St. Patrick's. David drew closer and saw an armless
man with long, straggly hair concentrating on the ground in
front of him. His interest aroused, David edged his way to
the front of the throng. The man was painting a portrait of
Christ on the sidewalk, using nothing but his feet. There
were mutterings of genuine awe as the artist dipped his toes
into the pigment and applied it with a graceful movement
of his leg.

David tossed a five-dollar bill on the growing pile of money
and hailed a cab.

The boy is awakened by the pungent aroma of chorizo and fresh-brewed coffee. He throws back the heavy hand-sewn quilt and quickly changes from Donald Duck pajamas into a T-shirt and jeans. The living room is strangely quiet for a Saturday. There are breakfast dishes in the sink, but otherwise the house is deserted.

"Grandma, where are you?!"

"Here, mijito," she calls from the back yard. "Aquí estoy."

The boy pads out into the garden, and the sudden wash of sunlight makes him rub the sleep from his eyes. His grandmother is squatting in a corner of the yard, her hands covered by thick cotton gloves.

"What are you doing?" he asks.

"Plantando un árbol," she tells him. "Planting a tree." She always speaks to him in English and Spanish.

"What for?"

"So it can grow big and tall like you. And when it gives fruit, you can help me pick it and I'll make a big bowl of your favorite guacamole. Venga, help me do it."

She takes the spade and patiently shows him how to scoop out the dirt. Then she lets him hold the sapling, and together they anchor it into the soil. The boy likes the feel of the damp earth on his hands as he forms a little crater around the slender trunk.

"Did you plant trees when you were a little girl, Grandma?"

"Sí, mijo. We had muchos árboles. We had a big hacienda with enough land to plant a thousand trees. Run and bring me the hose, por favor."

"Did you really plant a thousand trees?" he asks as he watches her water the baby avocado.

"No," she says with a weary chuckle. "But we had limones and plums and apples . . ."

"And avocados?"

"Oh yes. Muchos aguacates. When the revolution came, me and your Tia Rosa helped bury all our money and gold in a big hole in the ground to hide it from the bandidos. Then we covered it up and planted a tree just like this one to mark the place."

"Why?"

"So that Pancho Villa's men couldn't find it and use it to buy guns."

The boy has seen bandidos in the movies. The idea of his grandmother hiding treasure from such formidable bad guys is utterly fantastic.

"Then what happened?"

"Your grandfather brought us to California." She put the hose in his hand. "Here, you water now."

"Did you go back and get the gold?"

His grandmother is quiet for a while. When she speaks again, her voice has a dreamy quality that he has never heard before.

"Your tia went back, many years ago, but she couldn't find it." She shrugs. "Maybe the bandidos found it, eh? Quién sabe."

"Grandma?"

"Yes, mijito."

"Can we go back and look for the gold together?"

"Your grandma is too old for such adventures," she says, slowly shaking her head. Then she looks at him and brightens. "Pero cuando tú seas un hombre, puedes ir a buscarlo."

"What did you say, Grandma?"

"When you grow up to be a big, strong man, you can go look for it yourself."

The boy is so excited that he drops the hose, and it sprays into the air like a shimmering fountain.

"And if I find the gold, can I keep it?"

"Yes, mijito," she says, hugging him with all her might. "It will be yours, all yours."

Guy Garcia is also the author of the novel *Obsidian Sky* and a children's book, *Spirit of the Maya*. He has contributed to the fiction anthologies *Iguana Dreams, Pieces of the Heart,* and *Paper Dance: 55 Latino Poets*. A staff writer at *Time* for 12 years, where he wrote or contributed to several cover stories and covered politics, culture, and the arts, Garcia's journalism has also appeared in *The New York Times, Rolling Stone, Men's Journal, The Face, Harper's Bazaar,* and *Latina*. Garcia, who moved to New York from his native California in 1980, holds a bachelor's degree in political science from University of California at Berkeley, where he graduated Phi Beta Kappa, and a master's degree in journalism from Columbia University. Garcia was inducted into PEN in 1994 and is the winner of the 1994 Pluma de Plata, awarded by the Mexican government for the best travel story by a foreign writer. He lives in New York City.

California Fiction titles are selected for their literary merit and for their illumination of California history and culture.

Forthcoming titles: